DANIEL PATTERSON

ONE CHANCE

A Thrilling Christian Fiction Mystery Romance

Praise for Daniel Patterson's debut novel, One Chance

...kept me up all night but well worth the late hour endured!
— Jean Sago, Amazon Reviewer

...so intricately interwoven, and brilliantly written, that I was turning pages as fast as I could until 4 AM.
— Julia Busch, Amazon Reviewer

...the right amount of mystery, crime drama, faith and love.
— S. Bacon, Amazon Reviewer

This was a great Christian mystery. I was interested from the first sentence to the last.
— Marie Brockman, Amazon Reviewer

Finally a well written Christian mystery. The characters are totally believable. Plenty of suspense and action.
— Gail C Baker, Amazon Reviewer

Penelope Chance is a rare breed of policewoman. She has a heart but knows no matter what her feelings are, she has to do what is right.
— Pat Peregrin, Amazon Reviewer

This is a powerful story about faith, and a great mystery. Officer Penelope Chance trusts her life to be directed by God. She asks for his guidance in every step she takes.
— Ms Margaret, Amazon Reviewer

... I really enjoyed the way the author tied mystery, romance an down to earth living all together. Well worth your time.

— Dee Irene, Amazon Reviewer

This book was wonderful. The way that she went before the Lord for everything...in her personal and business life. She was a great example of how we should live our lives.

— Marcie Haskins, Amazon Reviewer

Superbly brilliant story from beginning to end with plenty of action and twists in between.

— James G. Davis
Author, Search and Rescue: Christy's Mission

I really enjoyed the mystery and the presence of God!

— Jen, Amazon Reviewer

Powerful Christian mystery.

— Stacy B. Whaley, Amazon Reviewer

I enjoy mysteries and this one was challenging to figure out.

— Jean Wallace, Amazon Reviewer

This book had lots of twist that kept me turning the pages, with strong Christian values that made my soul soar. Who says you can't have both.

— Dent, Amazon Reviewer

ALSO AVAILABLE FROM DANIEL PATTERSON

THE DEVIL'S GAME

A CHRISTIAN FICTION SUSPENSE THRILLER

One Chance: A Thrilling Christian Fiction Mystery Romance

Cover and internal design by Kenneth Gorden
Background photo © Natalia Lukiyanova

ISBN-13: 978-1481041270
ISBN-10: 1481041274

Second edition — March 2014

10 9 8 7 6 5 4 3 2

This second edition of One Chance is dedicated to the readers and reviewers of the first edition. Thank you for helping me improve upon Penelope's story. I am truly grateful!

ACKNOWLEDGMENTS

My father taught me at an early age that God would always be there when I needed Him, and He always has been. He brought an amazing group of people into my life to help complete the book you are holding in your hands. And now I have the honor and privilege of thanking those people here.

I remain deeply grateful to James G. Davis, without your inspiration and direction this story never would have been told. Thank you!

To fellow writer and author Shawn Wells, thank you for your help, support, and guidance.

To my editor extraordinaire Linda Hull, thank you for helping to make Penelope's story even better. I took most, but not all of your suggestions, therefore any mistakes are mine alone.

To my friends who have always been there for me (you know who you are), thank you for helping me celebrate the good times and getting me through the tough times.

A very special thank you to Meeghn and Michael, for always being there.

To Dina, Sue, Ziad and Allan, thank you for keeping me on track.

To my mom, dad, and sister, thank you for your unconditional love and support.

To all my readers, thank you for your support, I am truly blessed to have you.

Most importantly, I want to thank God for always being there when I needed Him.

ONE
CHANCE

CHAPTER 1

OFFICER PENELOPE CHANCE leaned back in her chair, and pulled her long, honey blond hair into a high ponytail. It was a quarter after seven and she had just finished the paperwork for the vandalism case at Little LuLu's sandwich shop on Orange Avenue. Two young men had been harassing the owners on and off since the shop opened three weeks before. Last night they broke a window and spray painted swastikas on the front door. Not the type of crime their little community saw a lot of.

Although Ben and LuLu Weinberg, the shop owners, were quiet and subtle, their detractors were not. Subtlety is rarely a trait displayed by people ruled by hate. The teens who tagged the shop bragged about doing their part to 'pure' the community. Penelope shook her head. Franklin, Florida, was a small town of about six thousand people. The population was growing due to their proximity to Gainesville and the pristine small-town atmosphere. This growth had revitalized the Main Street neighborhood, which was good for the town, but it brought some challenges.

Judge Dirksen would hear the case on Monday and Penelope was confident the two young vandals would face a fine and be sentenced to community service—beginning with helping with the cleanup of the sandwich shop and the installation of a new window. Maybe spending some 'quality time' with Ben and LuLu would show them that these shop owners were normal, hardworking people who made a delicious turkey sub and deserved respect.

Dear Lord, Penelope prayed silently. *Thank You for allowing me to serve the good people of this town and bring peace to my community. Help me be content with my job and my life and leave final judgment up to You. Amen.*

With the exception of a double homicide twenty-three years ago, nothing big happened in tiny Franklin, Florida. The Franklin Police Department employed one chief, six officers and one dispatcher. That was more than enough in this quiet, primarily rural area of the state. Most of Penelope's cases were relatively minor incidents. In spite of her prayers, the truth was that sometimes she wished something bigger would cross her desk, something to get her blood pumping and give her brain a good workout.

Just then the phone rang. Judy, the dispatcher, had already left for the day, so Penelope answered while shuffling paperwork around. "Franklin Police Department. This is Officer Chance."

"Hello ma'am," the man said, "I need to report a stolen car."

Another one? Penelope thought. "Okay," she said. "Let's start with your name and a description of the car, okay?"

"My name is Kyle Fredericks," the caller said. "My car is a burgundy, 2010 Buick Regal."

Penelope jotted down Kyle Fredericks' information and asked for the address. Mr. Fredericks was at home on East River Street. Penelope told the man she would be there in a few minutes to start an investigation and write up a report. She wrote down the time of the call. *Seven thirty in the evening.*

Penelope wondered if this had anything to do with the biggest case of the week. Mrs. Briggs' unlocked car had been stolen in the early hours this morning. There had been no witnesses because theft happened in the middle of the night. After assuring Mrs. Briggs that the Police Department would do everything in their power to get her car back, Penelope had spent most of the morning driving around town, looking for the cherry red 2005 Buick LeSabre, but it was nowhere to be found—nowhere within her jurisdiction, anyway. With no choice left, she had called the Florida Highway Patrol and issued a BOLO for the car.

Penelope radioed the other officers on duty to tell

them she was taking this call and headed out to her cruiser. Her shift was nearly over, but Fredericks lived on the same side of the county as she did. She would check out the scene, take the cruiser home and do the paperwork there. Penelope had a feeling this evening wasn't going to come out the way she expected. The sense that a change was just around the corner was almost a tangible thing.

* * *

Mr. Fredericks was waiting on his porch as Penelope stepped out of her cruiser and walked across the neatly manicured front yard. Fredericks was an older man with graying hair getting thinner on top. The Florida sun had baked the man's skin to a deep brown, and his teeth showed whiter for it as he smiled at Penelope.

As she strode up the lawn to greet the man, Penelope noticed the lack of broken glass in the driveway where Fredericks had said the car had been taken. So, the car was either unlocked or whoever stole it had been able to bypass the lock somehow.

"Mr. Fredericks? I'm Officer Chance," she said, offering her hand. "When did you notice your car was missing?"

The man shook Penelope's hand and replied, "Just about a minute before I called you. My wife and I were planning to see an eight-thirty movie in Gainesville and when we came out to get in the car, it was gone."

"Car unlocked?"

"Yes ma'am, it was." He hesitated and looked a bit guilty. "We never really had to..." he added.

"Did you go near the driveway at all?" Penelope asked, taking out her little pad and a pen.

"No ma'am, I didn't," Fredericks answered. "As soon as I saw the car was gone, I went back inside and called the Police."

"Okay. When did you last see your car here?" Penelope asked.

The man thought for a moment and then said, "Must have been about six when I got home from work tonight. The wife and I had dinner and afterwards we decided to go to a movie. But when it came time to leave we had no car."

After jotting down a few notes and facts, Penelope asked, "Did you hear your car's engine start up? Another vehicle? Anything like that?"

Mrs. Fredericks, shorter than her husband and a little rounder but just as deeply tanned, had walked out to them as they talked. Mr. Fredericks looked at his wife. "I didn't. Did you, honey?" he asked her.

She shook her head as Penelope wrote some more.

"Is it possible," Penelope asked, "that one of your neighbors may have seen or heard something?"

Mrs. Fredericks said, "Mrs. Fitch across the street might have seen something. She sees almost everything that goes on in the neighborhood."

"That so?"

The woman nodded and whispered in a conspiratorial tone. "She's retired and has nothing else to do, you know."

Penelope nodded. "Okay, I'll go talk to her and see if she can help. Let me look over your driveway first."

She looked up and down the paved driveway, and along the sides in the grass. Nothing. There might have been an impression where the grass was bent over. If it was, it was too obscured to be of any use.

She smiled at the Fredericks, thanked them and turned around to walk across the street to another neat little house with a front porch and lace curtains.

Mrs. Fitch opened the door before Penelope had the chance to knock. "You're here about the car thief?" she said through the screen door, her dark skinned face serious under a tidy gray wig.

"Yes ma'am," said Penelope.

"You want my name first? It's Carmella Fitch. I've lived here for fifty-five years, twenty of them alone since my husband passed on."

"Thank you, Mrs. Fitch. Did you see someone take the Fredricks' car?"

"Yes I did. I seen it all. About seven-fifteen a big white van with no windows in the back come down the street and pulled up in front of the Fredericks' house. A young man got out and went up to the Fredericks' car. He knew what he was doin'—a real professional, because in less than a minute, he had that car started and was gone and the white van took off after him.

"Can you give me a description of this young man?" Penelope asked, confident that Mrs. Fitch certainly would.

She nodded, "Sure I can, officer. I guess him to be about nineteen or twenty years old and just about six feet tall. He was very thin with dark hair. Didn't get a good look at his face, but he looked to be a white boy with some Hispanic parentage. Probably from his momma."

Penelope wrote down the description in her little notepad. "Did you happen to get the license number of the van, Mrs. Fitch?"

"Well, of course I tried to, but I didn't because everything happened too fast. Plus I was kind of stunned from looking at the boy's chest."

"Why is that?" Penelope asked, her pen pausing.

"Well, it was the strangest thing," Mrs. Fitch said. "He was wearing a woman's brassiere outside of his t-shirt. Big pink one and it looked as if he had stuffed it up with something."

Penelope looked at her questioningly.

A stern expression wrinkled Mrs. Fitch's brow. "I know what you must be thinking, officer Chance," she said. "But I'm telling you what I saw. I'm a Baptist and I do not drink."

"Oh, I'm not doubting your word, ma'am," Penelope said. "But you have to admit it just seems very odd."

"That's what I thought, too," Mrs. Fitch replied. "All kinds of people moving in these days and not a thing anyone can do about it. I just hope our property values don't go down."

She thanked Mrs. Fitch for taking the time to speak with her, went back to her cruiser and headed back toward Main Street and the Police station. She hadn't gone more than a block when she received a radio call from Florida Highway Patrol's dispatch to head over to the town clinic and interview the victim of an attempted murder.

Penelope asked them to repeat it before she believed it.

Finally, a challenging case. She was anxious to get started on it. Until she heard who the victim was!

CHAPTER 2

THE LAST CHANCE Tavern was just that for Doug Foster. The last opportunity to get a drink at the end of his day—he didn't keep liquor in his home because he felt that was a sign of being an alcoholic. The tavern was at the south end of Main Street, just before he had to make a right turn onto Paradise Road that would take him through orange groves and pasture land to his rural home. Doug could never resist the urge to stop in for that one more beer, even though he knew it would more likely be four or five. Sometimes he lost count of how many he had. Tonight would be one of those times. Come the wee hours of the morning, his pickup would be the only vehicle left in the parking lot.

He always stopped in here before he began the five-mile drive home. Most people would have enjoyed the scenery on this route—plenty of trees, with a field or two here and there. But Doug hated it. The sheer abundance of flora and fauna never failed to bore him near to death. And there was the empty lot just before the Southside Bridge. It never failed to mock him.

The Southside Bridge was the only bridge in town that crossed the Franklin River, which was really nothing more than a sixty-five foot wide creek. Franklin, as small as it was, never had the money to build another bridge. There really wasn't a need. The orange grove and the ranch belonged to people who lived in the neighboring town of Lakeview where the processing plants were located so that most of that traffic went the other direction. One bridge was all Franklin needed and so Doug's route home from the Pruett auto repair shop was the same every day.

In reality, the drive didn't take long—it just seemed that way because he disliked it so much. What Doug hated most about it was that he had no choice in the matter. He didn't have much choice in anything these days. Five years ago he and Camille bought that little farm house specifically because it was on a nice, quiet piece of land. Then three years later she divorced him, took half his money, took their three year old son and ran off with another man. Two years gone and he hadn't seen her since. He was stuck out there all alone with an upside down mortgage and one route home. And his route took him past The Last Chance.

Doug got out of his 1956 midnight-blue Ford F-100

pickup truck, the realistic flame job on the side catching the light from the tavern's neon signs. He walked across the parking lot and into the tavern where he was planning to drink his problems away for another night, never seeing the damage on the front of his truck. Shattered headlight. Broken plastic.

Sometimes even the best-laid plans just don't come out right.

CHAPTER 3

SINCE GAINESVILLE WAS only a twenty-minute drive and housed three large hospitals, Franklin didn't require a hospital of its own. The victim in the attempted murder had been taken to the town clinic where Doctor Jacob Gordon had everything he needed, most of the time, for anything from flu shots and dog bites, to broken arms. Patients needing surgery or more advanced care would be sent to Grace Memorial Hospital in Gainesville.

When officer Chance walked in the front door of the clinic, she headed straight for the exam rooms at the rear of the building. Doctor Jacob heard her footsteps echoing on the tiled floor and came out to see who was there. He bumped into her as he rounded the corner.

"I got the call a couple minutes ago. I came right over," she said. "Is Pete going to be okay?"

"His injuries are beyond what I can deal with here in the clinic," he replied with concern in his voice. "I've stabilized him. An ambulance is on its way to transfer him to Grace Memorial. He's in Exam Room Two, on the left."

Penelope steeled herself and slipped into police officer mode. "Can he talk?" She started to walk past him and Jacob grabbed her arm.

"He doesn't need any more stress right now..."

"We need to know who did this, Jacob. I need to talk to him while I can. In case...in case I can't talk to him later."

Jacob sighed. "I'll give you a few minutes. Penny, he's beat up really bad. I barely recognized him."

"Thanks for the warning," she said with a nod.

In a few quick strides, Penelope was at the door of Exam Room Two. She knocked lightly, opened the door and stepped in. Pete Lamb lay in the bed looking as if he'd lost a fight with a couple of pit bulls and a rabid alligator. He was nearly unrecognizable under all the cuts, scrapes, bruises and swelling on his face and upper body. And Penelope suspected that wasn't the worst of it.

"Hiya Pete," Penelope said, forcing a cheerful tone into her voice. "Rough night?"

"You could say that," Pete replied in a voice muffled by swollen lips.

Penelope approached the bed. She could smell alcohol on him. "Want to tell me what happened?"

One of Pete's eyes was swollen shut. He closed the other one now and swallowed thickly. "Told Doctor Gordon already. Doug. He tried to kill me."

"Doug?" she asked.

"You heard me," Pete said. "Doug Foster."

"Are you absolutely sure?" Penelope asked, too shocked to believe it.

Pete opened that one pale blue eye again and regarded Penelope. "There's only one truck like that in this town," he said.

"Did you see Doug driving it?"

"It was dark," said Pete. "But you know he don't loan that truck to nobody."

Penelope said, "It's important, Pete. Did you see Doug in the truck?"

"He hit me from behind. I was walking on County Road just up from The Last Chance. We all know who's at The Last Chance every night."

"Yeah, I do. You're sure it wasn't just an accident?" she asked. She had to remain objective.

"Not an accident," Pete said slowly. "Hit me the first time, knocked me in the middle of the road. Then he turned around and came at me again. Had to roll off the road in the ditch where he couldn't get at me." After a brief pause and a few ragged breaths he added, "I know he's a drunk like me. Hell, I bought him a beer just the other day. Why does he hate me now, Penny?"

"Trust me, Pete, he doesn't hate you," Penelope

answered, but even as she said it doubt nagged at the back of her mind. She took a deep breath and sighed as she moved toward the door. "I'll go now and make out the report. Doctor Gordon has an ambulance coming to take you over to Grace Memorial to get you checked out good."

"Sorry, Penny. Wish I could tell you it was somebody else."

"Thanks, Pete. But all I want is the truth, no matter what it is," Penelope added quietly as she left the room.

In the hallway she wrapped her arms around the Doctor and kissed him tenderly on the lips. They had been engaged for a little while now, and the day he had finally asked her was still one of the greatest moments of her life. She thanked God often for letting him come into her life. "You'll keep me updated on Pete's condition...?"

"Is that you, Penelope Chance?" A woman in her nightgown, slippers and a tattered robe stained with blood stormed toward them from the waiting room. "Why are you standing there smooching that doctor when you should be out arresting Doug Foster for trying to kill my brother?"

It was Patty Lamb, Pete's older sister.

Officer Bill Peterson followed Patty into the corridor. "Sorry Penelope. Didn't know you were back here."

Patty was fifty-eight years old and had never married. Patty had lived in the family home her entire life, taking care of her parents when they became elderly and then living alone after they both passed on. Pete had moved in with her a few years back when he lost his job.

Dr. Gordon took over with his usual diplomacy. "Miss Lamb, let me talk to you about your brother's condition while the officers work on their report." He steered her toward the exam room.

"Sorry again, Penelope," Bill said.

Penelope brushed it off. "Was she a witness?"

Bill shook his head. "No, Patty said she went looking for Pete when he didn't come home for supper and she found him in the ditch. He gonna be alright?"

"Jacob is sending him to Grace Memorial. Ambulance should be here any minute."

"That bad?"

"That bad," Penelope agreed.

"I guess Patty is going to want to go with him..."

"I'm sure. You wait here to see if there's room for her in the ambulance. If not, give her a ride."

"Will do," said Bill.

"I'm heading back to the station now," Penelope said. "Start the report."

"The station?" he questioned.

"The station," she said firmly. "You keep me updated."

"Of course," he said.

She'd been right. It was going to be a long night.

CHAPTER 4

WHILE SHE DROVE back to the police station, Penelope prayed silently. *Dear Lord, if it is Your will, please let this all be a big mistake.*

Somewhere deep inside, however, she had a feeling she might not get the answer she was hoping for.

Pray for sun, but bring an umbrella, she reminded herself. If Doug had done this, like Pete said, then Penelope would have no choice but to do her job.

She just wouldn't like it.

* * *

Twenty minutes later, as she sat at her computer filling out the preliminary report, her eyes kept going to the spot where she had written *Victim didn't see the driver.* It was a small relief to know that Pete hadn't actually seen Doug behind the wheel of that truck. But that didn't really matter. As Pete said, Doug never let anyone else drive his prized truck. She knew who the driver could be, as well as anyone else in town. Not wanting it to be so wasn't going to change reality.

She needed to put all this aside for a moment. She wouldn't have an update on Pete's condition for another couple of hours and she figured that was enough time.

So Penelope returned her attention to the case of the stolen Buicks. No witnesses for the first one, but a good witness for the second. Both cars had been unlocked. That wasn't unusual in a town where nearly everyone knew, and mostly trusted, each other. But it meant no physical evidence like broken glass with blood left at the scene.

The description of the suspect, however, was what kept going through her mind. She tried to imagine a tall, thin, possibly Hispanic young man wearing a stuffed bra over his t-shirt. No matter how hard she tried, she couldn't help chuckling at the thought. Who would want to draw that kind of attention to themselves as they went out to steal Buick after Buick?

She logged onto the state's Department of Motor Vehicles website and searched for all red Buicks owned by residents of Franklin. There were six. Disregarding the two that were stolen she was still left with four possible future thefts.

That was good, but now she needed to figure out which one was likely to be the next. There must be something about the first two, other than the color, that made them targets for the thief.

Looking back at both reports, she tried to find similarities between them. The first thing that caught her eye was the addresses of the victims. Neither was more than three blocks from Main Street. That could be what had made them easy targets. Additionally, each house was also near an intersection with a side street. Of the possible remaining targets, she saw only one more that fit the same criteria. Anthony Abernathy, up near Maple Avenue.

Makes sense, she thought. From Main Street all the thief would have to do is go west and in less than ten minutes he could be heading north on US 301. Not only would that lead the thief out of town, but it also led toward Gainesville.

Penelope went into the break room to get a cup of coffee. As she was adding sugar to her cup, officer Jim Saunders came in preceded, as always, by his magnificent handlebar mustache. "You're back?" he said.

"Jim, your powers of observation are truly amazing," she said.

"Did you get to see Pete? He gonna be all right?"

Penelope turned serious again. "Jacob isn't sure. He sent him to Grace Memorial to check for internal injuries. He'll let me know."

Jim boosted himself up to sit on the edge of the break room counter top. "Did you get to talk to him? Does he know who did it?"

"It was someone in Doug Foster's truck."

"That would be Doug Foster," Jim said. "Wow!"

"It was his truck," Penelope said firmly. "Pete didn't see who was driving it."

"Right," said Jim. "That would have been Doug Foster. You want me to take that the lead on this one?" Jim asked her.

Penelope shook her head. "I've got it. For now. Hey, we have a witness in the stolen car case." Penelope told him about the description Mrs. Fitch had given of the suspect in his case.

Saunders laughed and then offered a possible explanation. "This guy sounds as though he might be in college," he said.

A light came on in Penelope's mind. "Thank you, Jim," she said. "That just may be what I'm looking for."

Jim's expression changed and he hopped off the counter top. Penelope turned around and saw Chief Curtis Jackson standing behind her with a scowl on his deep brown face. At six-foot-two inches and well over two hundred pounds, that was a lot of scowl.

"Officer Chance," the Chief began, and Jim Saunders suddenly thought of something he had to do somewhere else. Penelope knew she was in trouble. "Did I just hear that you had a lead on a suspect in this hit and run?"

"Yes, sir."

"And yet you stand here before me, drinking a cup of coffee instead of picking him up for an interview. I figured you'd be on it like a fat kid on a cupcake, seeing as how you're always bellyaching about how small your caseload is."

Penelope slumped and fought back the sudden tears that threatened to form in her eyes. "I'm not sure if I'm the right one for this case, sir," she said quietly.

Chief Jackson grabbed a chair from the break room table set and scraped it across the floor. He settled himself into it and the metal frame creaked in protest. Under the furrowed brow of his bald-head, his face softened visibly. He motioned for Penelope to sit as well.

"Penelope," he began, "I gave you a job here, once upon a time, because you were the best of all the applicants. You're smart, you're dedicated, and you honestly care about the people of Franklin. Shoot, you grew up here. It wouldn't sit right if I gave a case this big to anyone else."

"Thank you, sir, but—"

"I know," the Chief replied. "I've lived in Franklin all my life, too, and I'm well aware that you grew up with both of them. That's the other reason you have the case."

"I don't follow," Penelope said, honestly confused.

"Penelope, you have a heart of gold," the Chief told her. "That's what people love about you and why they respect you. I know you can do this because you have the determination to get to the bottom of it for both of their sakes. You won't play favorites. You'll be fair, and you'll be honest."

It was good to know where she stood with her boss. Took some of the pressure off.

"I guess the biggest thing is that I'm not looking forward to the arrest," she said.

"I know, Penelope, and I appreciate how hard this is going to be for you," the Chief told her. "I also know that you are the only one I've got who can handle this the right way. Oh, the rest of my guys are good but you're better. It's that whole honest girl scout thing you've got going on."

"I put my faith in God, sir," Penelope said. "It makes me who I am."

"See now, right there is what I mean. This case is going to require a lot of faith and trust," the Chief said as he rose from his chair. "When it comes to that, you are the one I trust. Now instead of worrying about these stolen cars you need to bring Doug in for questioning."

"Well, sir. About that. I was thinking I'd just take him to my house for tonight."

Chief Jackson turned around and looked at her as if she'd spoken in Ancient Greek.

"We know that his vehicle was involved, but we don't know that he was—"

"Now, Penny..."

"Chief, if I bring him in for questioning, he's likely to shut down." She hurried on, preventing Chief Jackson from interrupting her. "I'm off for the next two days. We'll get a warrant from Judge Dirksen tonight to impound his vehicle for processing. I can have Doug stay with me to make sure he doesn't get into any trouble."

She paused to see what effect her words were having. "Please, Chief, let me see what I can find out. He'll open up to me."

Curtis thought for a moment and sighed, relenting. "Okay, but only for the weekend. If anything changes, if something else comes up, I'll expect you to be the one to bring him in without delay."

"Yes sir, I will. Thank you, sir," Penelope said.

"Well, what are you waiting for, officer Chance?"

Penelope hurried out of the break room before he changed his mind and headed for the door.

"Don't make me regret this," the Chief called after her.

"I won't, sir," she said. *God willing*, she thought.

Before she left, Penelope asked Saunders to sit in an unmarked car on the corner of High Street and Maple Avenue to keep an eye on Mr. Abernathy's victory-red 2010 Buick LaCrosse. There was no way for her to know when the culprit might come for this car, but she didn't want to gamble on having another red car to look for on top of everything else.

CHAPTER 5

ELEVEN O'CLOCK: DOUG staggered out of The Last Chance Tavern after having one too many. Well, many too many was more like it. As he stumbled across the small dirt parking lot to his pickup, he noticed officer Penelope Chance leaning against the hood of her police cruiser.

"Heya Penny," Doug said, his words having taken on that distinctive alcohol slur, "didja catch any crooks today?"

Penelope looked at Doug with more than a small amount of pity and thought about the events that led her lifelong friend down the path of destruction.

"Not yet," she answered Doug's question, the irony of it weighing heavy on her. "Been waiting for you to come out so that I can take you home. I don't want to bring you in for DUI."

"Nah ah ahhh! Ain'tgonnahap'n," Doug drawled. "I'm plannin' t' sleep in my truck 'til mornin' b'fore I go home."

Penelope said, "I can't let you do that, Doug. In fact, I'm going to take you to my house. You can stay the night. We'll talk in the morning."

"Thanks, buddy," Doug said with a cheerful smile, patting Penelope's shoulder. "I 'preciate that Penny. My gardienanjshul, tha'swutsha are."

Penelope opened the door and let him climb into the back of the cruiser. The other officers would take the truck once she was far enough away so that Doug wouldn't see them do it. Penelope had already seen the front end and snapped a few pictures.

As Doug settled into the back seat, already half asleep, Penelope gripped the steering wheel hard and headed the cruiser out onto the road. It was going to be a short night, and a difficult conversation in the morning, when she told a more sober Doug that he was the prime suspect in an attempted murder.

CHAPTER 6

AT NINE O'CLOCK on Saturday morning, Doug's eyes opened. His eyes were blurry from drink and sleep. The memory of last night was all fuzzy around the edges. He didn't even remember making it home. Not the first time anyway. His eyes focused slightly. Not home, but in a familiar place. How did he get to Penny's house, he wondered.

After a quick trip to the bathroom, where he splashed cold water on his face and ran his wet hands through his long brown hair, he trudged into the kitchen to look for something to settle his stomach.

He saw Penelope seated at the small table eating eggs, bacon and toast. There was another plate of the same set out with a large mug of black coffee next to it.

"What's going on, Penny?" Doug asked, seating

himself at the table.

"Having some breakfast," she replied.

Doug sat down and grinned. He said, "No, I mean why did you bring me to your house last night?"

"Haven't spent time with my best buddy in a while, so it seemed like a good idea." Penelope said. It was a lie with just enough truth in it so that she hoped Doug would buy it, at least long enough to have breakfast.

"You are sure it wasn't that you didn't want me driving drunk?" Doug asked as he stuffed most of an egg in his mouth and washed it down with the coffee.

"Yeah. That too," Penelope said as she brought her plate to the sink. She poured herself another cup of coffee. "I need to talk to you about something when you finish. I'll be in the living room."

Penelope left the kitchen and sat down in one of the two overstuffed recliners in the room.

Lord, she prayed, *please let him understand and not be upset with me.*

That last part seemed a little selfish once it was out there. *You know what I mean*, she added.

Several minutes later Doug came into the room and sat across from Penelope on the sofa. "Okay, look," he said, "you know where I live. There's no cars, no traffic. No way for me to get in trouble. I was going to sleep it off in the truck anyway..."

Penelope blew out a long breath. "We had an attempted murder in Franklin last night."

The surprise on Doug's face was honest and genuine. And Penelope took note of that.

"What?" he asked. "What are you talking about? Who was it? Are they okay? Who did it?"

"Pete Lamb is the victim and we don't know if he's going to be okay," Penelope said, ignoring the rest of Doug's questions for now. "His injuries were pretty extensive. Jacob had to transfer him to Grace Memorial."

"Why would somebody try to kill Pete? Why would anyone do that? He never hurt nobody."

"That's what we'd like to know," Penelope replied.

"So what does this have to do with me?" he asked, not sure he wanted to know.

Lord, help me choose the right words, Penelope asked, sighing and rubbing her eyes. *She hadn't slept much last night.*

"Pete swears it was your truck that hit him."

There, Penelope thought. *That gets a large cat out of a tiny bag.*

"*My* truck?" Doug said, stunned, his voice rising in pitch. "Uh-uh. No way. Pete said that?"

"Do you really need me to answer that?"

Doug sagged back onto the couch. "Well, he's wrong, Penny! It was someone else!"

"It was your truck, Doug. I saw the damage on it myself. It's a pretty recognizable old truck with that custom paint job and all." She didn't mention the blood on the cracked headlight and grill.

The friends sat in uncomfortable silence for a few minutes that stretched out like hours.

"Well, I think I would remember something like that no matter how drunk I was."

"Pete swears it was your truck, Doug," Penelope told him. "Now you never lend that truck to anyone, do you? Everyone kind of knows that. It's your baby."

"Now, wait a second, Penny!"

Penelope held up a hand. "Hold on, hold on. You and me and Pete have been friends for a long time and I really can't stomach the idea that this was you—"

"That's because it wasn't me!" Doug interrupted.

"...and that's why I brought you here last night. We brought your truck in to process it for evidence. "

"So I'm under house arrest? Here in your house?"

Penelope shrugged her shoulders. "It's better than in the lock-up at the station which is where the Chief thinks you should be. I'm risking a lot for you by doing this, Doug. I'm asking you to stay here for a day or two, until we get this figured out."

Doug couldn't believe it. He shook his head again and again. "There has to be a mistake. I don't remember hitting anybody. Or anything!"

"You're sure, Doug? Maybe you thought you hit a deer or something?" Penelope was grasping at straws.

"No way," Doug said. "I'm one hundred percent certain I didn't hit anything last night. Not a deer, not a squirrel and sure as hell not a person!"

"How can you be so sure, Doug?"

"Because I wasn't that drunk before I got to The Last Chance, Penny. Sure, I had one beer with my supper at The Pizza Palace."

"Just one?"

"Yes. One. Then I went to Ricky's Pub for happy hour."

"You were at two bars last night?"

"Penny. Don't you judge me!"

"I'm not judging you. I need to ask these questions. This is serious."

"Sorry. Yes, I was at two bars last night. I had a few beers at Ricky's but mainly I was shooting pool. I didn't get drunk until I got to The Last Chance."

"And you didn't notice the damage to the front end of your baby when you left Ricky's?" Penelope didn't enjoy interrogating her best friend, but she needed to know what Doug remembered. "You're sure about that?"

"Yes," Doug said, frustrated. "You gotta believe me, Penny. After what we been through together I wouldn't lie to you. Not to you."

"I believe you, Doug. Only because you're such a bad liar," Penelope told him, managing a tight smile. "But I don't know if anyone else will."

"You'll have to make them believe me," Doug said.

"I'll do what I can."

* * *

While they were cleaning the dishes together, Penelope got a call from the Chief himself. Early that morning the thieves had indeed attempted to take Mr. Abernathy's car, just as Penelope had predicted. The Chief was calling from home to congratulate her on a job well done. On a weekend. Penelope suspected there was more to it than that.

"I'd like you to come in and finish up the paperwork, Penelope," he told her. "You've got the most information about this case."

"Uh, sure thing, Chief," Penelope answered, waiting for the other shoe to drop.

"How's your house guest?" Chief Jackson asked abruptly.

Just like she'd guessed, this was what the Chief really wanted.

Penelope told him that she had dropped the news on Doug and about his alibis.

"So I guess you have more than just the car theft paperwork to do today," he said. "You sure Doug is going to mind his manners and stay put while you come in to work?"

"I'm sure," she said, giving Doug a stern look. "He'll stay put."

She went upstairs to put on her uniform and her duty belt. The weight of it settled comfortably on her hips. After so many years it was almost part of her persona now. She used most of the equipment on it on a regular basis—handcuffs, flashlight holder, utility knife, and so on. But it had been a long, long time since she'd had to pull her service weapon, a Sigma .40 caliber automatic handgun. The strength she depended on to do her work didn't come from that.

CHAPTER 7

TWENTY MINUTES LATER Penelope was sitting in the interrogation room, questioning the main suspect in the case of the stolen cars. To Penelope's amusement the guy had been brought in wearing the ridiculously stuffed brassiere and no one had allowed him to remove it. The young man's name was Pedro Gonzales, originally from Miami, and he was taking classes at the University of Florida in Gainesville. The guy's partner, Sean Macos, was in the holding cell, waiting his turn to be interviewed.

"So," Penelope prompted Mr. Gonzales, "tell me why you and Sean were stealing red Buicks."

Pedro grinned at her. "What can I say? You got me. We're pledges for a fraternity. We had to do it for our initiation."

"Had to?" Penelope pressed.

Pedro shrugged. The stuffed brassiere jiggled.

"Which fraternity?" Penelope asked.

Pedro smiled and shook his head. "Can't tell you that."

"Okay," Penelope said. "See your friend Sean out there? I wonder if his loyalty is as strong as yours. I wonder whether he'll jump at the chance of pinning this all on you if I offer him a deal."

Pedro crossed his arms and grinned at her. "It's just a few old cars," he said.

"No," Penelope said. "It's actually felony grand theft auto, Mr. Gonzales. You'll lose your license, you'll be hit with some pretty hefty fines, and you'll be kicked out of school, but don't worry about not being able to live in the frat house. You can be our guest in one of our lovely correctional institutions for at least a year …"

"I wasn't the one driving."

"Still grand theft auto." Penelope stood. "I'm going to talk to Mr. Macos. Maybe he'll be a little more cooperative."

"And what if he is?" Pedro asked.

"Well, then," said Penelope. "Things could be very different for him. If he has no prior record he could be charged with just a misdemeanor…"

"I have no prior record…"

"…and if he cooperates fully and tell us where the cars are and they are recovered undamaged…"

"But if the cars are at the frat house…"

"Whoever is in possession of them will be summarily

arrested," finished Penelope.

"Then we'll never get in the fraternity," Pedro said glumly.

Penelope gave him her best 'Are you really that stupid?' look. "Yeah, Pedro. That's pretty much not going to happen no matter what, now. The best you can hope for now is not to spend a year in prison and since you don't want to cooperate I'm going to see if Sean will." She moved to the door.

"Wait!" Pedro said. "If anyone is not going to go to jail it's going to be me. It's the Sigma Beta Sigma fraternity! Brother George put us up to it."

Penelope took out her pad and pen. "Brother George?" she asked.

"George Flanagan. Do you want his phone number and email?"

"That would be helpful," Penelope said. She wrote down the information he gave her.

"What happens now?" Pedro asked.

"Now I talk to Sean," she told him. "See if your stories collaborate. If they do the two of you will spend a few hours in the holding cell while a couple of officers go and look for the cars. If they are recovered in decent condition and if everyone is sufficiently contrite and has sufficiently clean records and if the cars' owners agree, maybe, just maybe, no one will be charged. It will then be up to your school to decide what to do with you."

"That's a lot of ifs," said Pedro.

"It certainly is," Penelope agreed. She took him out of the interrogation room to the second holding cell.

Penelope interrogated Sean Macos and was rewarded with very similar results. Penelope called her contact at the Gainesville police department to give them the information and ask them to check out the frat house for the cars and Brother George.

Before she completed the call Jim Saunders began lurking in front of her desk. "What is it, Jim?" she asked as she hung up.

"Well," he drawled in his thick Georgian accent. "I'm not sure, but I'm thinkin' we may have a pair of runaways."

"How do you think we have a pair of runaways? You either do or you don't."

"Well, because it might be a kidnapping instead." He paused for dramatic effect.

"Do go on," she said.

"I think you know the girl, Penny. It's Missy Clark. Seen you in the park across the street talkin' to her and that Tommy Pruett, so I figured you might know what's goin' on."

"Yeah, I know those two. They're good kids, but in too much of a hurry to grow up."

"Parents say they haven't seen her since she left for school yesterday," Saunders said. "I already checked with Mr. Dobson down at the grocery store, where she works after school. He says she was there sure enough and left at seven thirty last evening. 'Course, he also seems to think she stole two hundred dollars from her register. He wasn't gonna say anything, but when he heard she might be missin' he thought it was better to say so."

Penelope was surprised. "Missy stole from her register? That doesn't sound right. She never seemed like the type to do that."

"All I know is he said her drawer came up two hundred dollars short and now her parents say they haven't seen her in more than a day."

"She won't answer her cell phone?"

"They didn't let her have one."

"Have Missy's parents tried calling her friends?"

"Yup. They all say they haven't seen her since school let out yesterday."

"You've talked to Tommy's parents?"

"Tommy's parents don't seem to be all that interested."

Typical, thought Penelope. "So how does any of this relate to a kidnapping?"

"Well," Jim said, "Tommy turned eighteen a couple of months ago. Missy is still seventeen."

"That's right," Penelope said.

"And her parents want her back and him thrown in jail," Jim said. "They're making a pretty big fuss about it on the phone calling him a kidnapper and a few other select things."

"Kidnapper!" Penelope exclaimed. "They're boyfriend and girlfriend..."

"I know, I know. It does seem kind of...excessive."

Penelope had to wonder at the foolish things young hearts did. "Let's find them first," she said. "Maybe we can sort this thing out."

"We don't have to like the law..."

"We just have to enforce it," Penelope finished for him. "Tell Missy's parents that we'll put an Amber alert out. Then get on the computer and check Missy's Facebook and Twitter pages to see if there's anything there to suggest were they went..." She stood and headed for the door. "I'm going to go check out Doug's alibis."

CHAPTER 8

PENELOPE'S ROUTE TO the Pizza Palace took her past the clinic. She saw Jacob's car, so she stopped to check Pete's condition. The door was locked and she rang the buzzer.

A few moments later, a serious faced Dr. Gordon opened the door. "Is this a medical emergency?" he asked.

"Yes, it is," she said with a lopsided grin.

He frowned at her. "What seems to be the problem, officer?"

"I'm suffering from withdrawal symptoms."

"Hmmm. Sounds like you have an addiction."

"I believe I do," she said.

"I do have a number of pamphlets on addiction here..." his lecture was cut off when Penelope wrapped her arms around him and kissed him firmly on the lips.

"An un-orthodox method of treatment sometimes

works surprisingly well," he admitted.

Penelope did not release him. "I believe I need one more treatment, Doc."

He kissed her and they lingered a bit longer this time.

"Better?" he asked when they parted.

"Much," she replied.

"Do you need another?"

Penelope pulled out of the embrace. "I think that would be counter-productive at this time," she said with a smile.

"May I suggest full time treatment beginning as soon as possible?"

"I do have a reservation for just such an arrangement," she said. "In the meantime, we need to get back to work."

"Agreed," he said. "I'm sure you're here to ask about Pete. He's critical, but stable. He's got a couple of broken ribs and a sprained wrist. The MRI showed no serious internal injuries but these kinds of things sometimes don't show up right away. They are going to keep him another day for observation just to be sure. If everything still checks out he could be released tomorrow morning."

Penelope closed her eyes. "Thank you, God."

"Thanks from me too, Lord," said Jacob. "The human body is an amazing creation. Pete was pretty drunk when he was hit and that means he was relaxed. I think that is what kept him from being more seriously hurt. Well, that and rolling into the ditch so that Doug couldn't hit him again."

Penelope's face darkened. "We don't know for sure that it was him, Jacob."

"Did you pick him up?"

"Yes."

"And he says he didn't do it, right?"

Penelope bristled at that. "Innocent until proven guilty, Jacob. Pete didn't see who was driving. I know it was Doug's truck, but he swears he didn't do it. And I believe him."

"Come on, Penny. Poor Pete is the town drunk only because he's a few years older and beat Doug to that position first."

Penelope switched into impartial cop mode. "I believe Doug is telling the truth. I talked to him this morning over breakfast. I'd know if he was lying."

"Over breakfast? At the station?"

"No," she said. "I brought him to my house to keep an eye on him. He's there now."

"I'm not really sure how I feel about that, Penny." The look that Jacob gave her spoke volumes.

"Jacob, come on. It's Doug. He's family." She touched his cheek gently. "You've got less than nothing to worry about." She hesitated and her eyes filled with tears. "I won't just give up on him. He's the closest thing I have to a real brother," Penelope said, almost tearfully.

Jacob embraced her. "I know you love him like a brother, Penny. And I trust you, I do...But you have to be ready for the very real possibility that he did do this to Pete. I just don't want you tangled up in that if that's what shakes out of this."

Penelope took a deep breath and pulled out of the embrace. "I have faith, Jacob. And it will keep me strong enough to deal with whatever happens. God will not throw me anything that He thinks I can't handle."

"He's thrown you an awful lot, Penny..."

She forced a smile. "And I've rejoiced in the good and learned from the bad. He's made me who I am today and I am grateful for every minute of it. And right now, I am going out there to do my job the best way I can. Dinner tonight?"

"You can count on it," Jacob said.

CHAPTER 9

PENELOPE'S FIRST STOP on her way to verifying Doug's story was The Pizza Palace. Greg and Sally Bernard, the owners of the place, had long ago tried to get a Pizza Hut franchise, but the big chain turned them down. So they had opened their own version under a slightly different name and it turned out to be a big hit.

It was the lunch rush, so to get some time to talk with the waitress, Mandy Blonkin, Penelope sat down and ordered a slice of pizza and a soft drink. Between serving other customers, Mandy told Penelope that she had worked a double the previous day and, yes, Doug came in at about five and, yes, he only drank one beer with his pizza. In fact, he didn't even finish it before he left forty-five minutes later. And he hadn't left her a tip. This final fact was given with a look that conveyed that

Penelope was expected to compensate for that since she was his friend. She did.

Next, Penelope went to Ricky's Pub over on the east side of town. It was established in 1982 with a beach theme when its owner Rick Ferrero returned from Spring Break full of inspiration and determination to spend his inheritance on bringing a little Key West style to his home-town rather than finishing his education. The gamble worked and the tiny pub was still thriving.

When Penelope arrived she found Ricky tending to a lunch crowd of twelve. All he could say was the place had done a banner business last night, what with it being Quiz Night and all, and there was no way he would be able to tell Penelope if his own mother had been in there.

She asked Ricky if she could get the surveillance footage from outside the bar for last night. Ricky looked a little sheepish and told her that the cameras out there hadn't worked in months. They were just there for show. So much for that idea! That would have at least told her if there was damage on Doug's truck before he left for The Last Chance Tavern.

Penelope declined Ricky's offer for a fish sandwich and fries and went back out to her squad car. The next step was to head over to The Last Chance Tavern and verify Doug's alibi there. Before she started the car her text message alert sounded. She opened the text. It was from Doug.

EUGHN.

Suddenly, she recognized their code word from when she and Doug were younger. EUGHN, the word on her cell phone screen, meant Extremely Urgent Get Here Now!

She jammed the cell phone back into its holder, got into her cruiser, turned the emergency lights on and headed for home.

CHAPTER 10

WITH CRUISER LIGHTS sending out flashes of red and blue, Penelope came to a screeching halt in her own driveway. Doug came running out to meet her even before the car stopped.

"I got here as fast as I could," Penelope said, her adrenaline level elevated. "What's up?"

Doug's eyes were wild and frantic. "Trevor is gone! He's missing—I can't find him!"

"Trevor is with Camille..."

Doug began racing around the front yard looking into the hedges. "Trevor! Where are you?" He turned around and yelled at Penelope, "Help me find my little boy, Penny! I don't know what I'll do if I can't find him! Please, Penny! Help me find Trevor!" he begged.

"Doug, you been drinking?"

Doug turned on her, angry. "I'm stone cold sober, Penny. Why when anything happens, do people ask me if I'm drunk?"

"Because truth is, Doug, you usually are." Penelope said. "Now calm down and tell me what's going on."

"Trevor was here and now he's missing!"

"How did Trevor get here? Where's Camille?"

Doug sat down on the front step of the porch and put his head in his hands. "Camille came by about half an hour after you left. I don't...I don't know how she knew I was here."

"You know how fast rumors fly in this town." Penelope told him. "By now I'm sure everybody knows you're at my house."

Doug nodded. He was no stranger to the rumors of the town.

"Anyway. She said she wanted to talk, said she wanted to work things out. Said a bunch of stuff, really. Then she said she had to get back to Gainesville and she asked me to keep Trevor until she came back. I was just so happy to see my son again, you know?"

"Why didn't you call and tell me about this?" Penelope asked.

Doug shrugged a shoulder. "I figured you'd be busy and I didn't want to bother you."

"I have been busy today, sure," Penelope said, some of her own frustration seeping into her voice, "but I need to know what's going on at my own house, Doug.

You understand the situation I've put myself in for you? I'm basically protecting you from an attempted murder charge right now."

"Fine, fine, Penny, I get it, but why are we wasting time with this when Trevor is missing?" Doug stood up again.

"What happened? How did he go missing?"

"I don't know! He's quick I guess! A couple of hours after Camille left, he was in the living room playing with his cars. I went in the bathroom for thirty seconds, I swear, no longer than that, and when I came out, I couldn't find him."

"He's probably hiding. Playing a game." Penelope stood as well. "Let's go through the house one room at a time," she suggested.

"Penny, I've looked everywhere! And I've looked around outside, and—"

"One more time, Doug," Penelope said again, "just so that I can be sure."

* * *

The search took only a few minutes, both inside and out, but Trevor was nowhere to be found. Penelope made a quick call to the station to get the officer on duty, Bill Peterson, to do a quick drive by Doug's house. After the phone call, Penelope insisted that Doug sit quietly on the couch. There was no sense in running around in a panic.

She asked him why he thought Camille had come back.

"She said she made a mistake and wants to come home to me," Doug replied.

The sound of desperate hope in her friend's voice broke Penelope's heart. Penelope thought the chances of Camille ever coming back to Doug were either slim or none. But she would never tell her friend that. "You know I've been praying for both of you, right?" Penelope told him.

Doug simply smiled in return. His faith had never been as strong as hers and sometimes she felt he was just humoring her when she spoke to him about God. She prayed about that too.

After a moment, Doug asked, "How's Pete doing?"

"He is in stable condition at Grace Memorial. He's got a few broken bones and now they are waiting to see if he has internal injuries."

Doug's hands fidgeted with each other. "I don't know what's going on, Penny. Pete's run over. Camille's back. Trevor's missing. None of it seems right."

"I know what you mean," Penelope said but very little of it made any sense. Camille coming back, at this moment, could not have been worse timing. She leaned over and offered Doug a hand. "We've got a few things to ask for, so let's get started."

Doug reluctantly accepted Penelope's hand.

She bowed her head and began, "Dear Lord, we are confident You already know what is happening here, so we ask that Pete be restored to good health. Let Your will be done, Lord."

"Please, God," Doug started as soon as Penelope finished, "I know I don't talk to you much but please let Penny figure out the truth of this situation. I'm sure You know who really did this wicked thing to Pete. And, Lord, please, ...my Trevor..."

"Lord, lead the lost child back to his father, we pray," Penelope finished for Doug. "We thank You for Your help, Lord. We know You help us in our worst moments. May we all be better through Your grace and Your guidance. Amen."

"Amen," Doug echoed. He wiped away a couple of tears.

Penelope smiled at him and went into the kitchen to set the coffee pot to brew. Now all they could do was wait for Peterson to arrive.

No sooner was the thought out of her head than she heard the car pulling into her driveway. Out of the window she could see officer Bill Peterson behind the wheel of the second police cruiser. And she could just see the top of a little blond mop of hair in the passenger seat.

"Thank you, Lord," she whispered. She turned to Doug with a smile. "Come on, buddy. You're gonna to want to see this."

Doug's eyes flew open wide and he jumped up and ran for the front door. He cleared the three front porch steps with one leap and swept his little boy into a tight embrace as the child laughed and squirmed in his father's arms. Tears ran down Doug's face again, joyful tears this time.

"Where'd you find him?" Penelope asked Bill.

"Right off of Paradise Road," Bill drawled. "Said he had to take his cats for a walk. Weirdest thing was, weren't no cats with him."

Penelope had to laugh. Bill didn't have any kids of his own. Apparently imaginary cats were too much for him to fathom.

Doug picked Trevor up in his arms and walked over to where the two deputies stood. "Thank you, Bill. Really. I don't know what I would have done if I'd lost him." He tasseled Trevor's hair and the little boy squealed as only five year old boys can.

Bill stared at Doug with a blank expression. "Right," he said finally. "Guess you're just having a rough weekend all the way 'round, ain'tya?"

Then he turned and went back to his cruiser. A moment later, he was driving away.

Doug closed his eyes and shook his head. He realized how the people in town had already made up their minds about him.

"Don't let it get to you, buddy," Penelope said to him. "The important thing is that we found Trevor. He's safe. It looks as if now I'm going to have two house guests instead of one for the next few days." She figured she could handle that, especially extra new one as happy as Trevor was, babbling non-stop to his father. They probably had a lot to catch up on, since Camille had kept Trevor away for so long.

"Doug, what's Camille's phone number?" she asked as they went back up the steps into the house.

"What's that?" Doug said, looking at Penelope.

"She had to leave you her phone number, right? I mean, when she dropped Trevor off and then had to leave again, she must have given you some way to get in touch with her?"

"Uh, no. She didn't. Sorry, Penny, I didn't even think about it until now." He tossed Trevor up in the air and caught him again, much to the delight of the young boy.

As Doug hugged Trevor to him again, the boy said in a singsong voice, "Five-five-five, one, zero-zero-eight."

Both Doug and Penelope stopped and stared at Trevor.

"What's that, little guy?" Doug asked him.

"Mama's phone number," Trevor answered. "Throw me again!"

Penelope got out her pad of paper from her shirt pocket. "Say it again Trevor, can you say it again?"

The boy repeated his song and Penelope punched it into her cell phone.

"Good job, big boy!" Doug praised his son.

Trevor laughed. "Throw me! Throw me!"

Doug did as his boy asked him, but spoke to Penelope at the same time. "What did you want to talk to Camille about?"

"Sorry, Doug, I have a few questions for her. It's all part of the investigation. Plus, it's just a good idea to have it, what with Trevor here, don't you think?"

Doug nodded but didn't look happy about it.

CHAPTER 11

FOR HALF AN hour the friends sat at the kitchen table remembering the days when Doug and Camille were married and Trevor was just a baby. Neither of them wanted to spoil what was left of the afternoon with any mention of what caused the divorce.

Penelope tried Camille's number a few times but got voicemail each time. She left two messages asking her to call back when she could.

"Did she say where she had to go off to so quickly?" she asked Doug.

"No, and I didn't ask, Penny. I'm just so happy to see Trevor again, you know? It's been so long."

Penelope watched Trevor playing on the living room floor with two plastic trucks and a stuffed dog, toys that he had apparently brought with him when Camille dropped him off.

"I know that look," Doug said to her. "What are you thinking, Penny?"

Penelope shook her head. "It's probably nothing. Just me being my usual police-self. The timing is just odd. Why now? Why this weekend, of all weekends, when you're in so much trouble?"

Doug blinked. "Penny, there's no way that Camille could have known about all this before she came."

"I know, I know. So like I said. Nothing. I'm just glad for you. Really. And I really hope things work out for you two."

Trevor ran out to them and reached his hands up to Doug to be picked up. Once he had settled himself in Doug's lap he asked, "Daddy, can I have a snack?"

Doug looked at Penelope.

"Sounds like a good idea to me," Penelope said. "I'm sure I've got something in my kitchen that a kid will eat. You and your Daddy go take a look. I've got to get back to work for an hour or two."

Trevor raced into the kitchen and Doug began to follow. Penelope pressed something into his hand. He looked and saw her car keys.

"I don't want you stranded with Trevor here. What if you have a milk emergency?" she said.

Doug grinned.

"This means I trust you, Doug."

"Thank you, Penny."

"Now don't let that boy fill up on junk. I want you to bring him to meet me and Jacob for dinner around seven tonight."

"Mmmmm! Cookies!" Trevor shouted from the pantry.

"I'd better get in there..." said Doug.

"Yeah," said Penelope. "I'm pretty sure I don't have any cookies." She left Trevor and Doug to explore the kitchen and went outside to call Jacob on her cell.

He answered the phone, "What's up, officer beautiful?"

"Hey doctor wonderful, I was wondering if you would mind having a couple of friends join us tonight for dinner."

"Not at all. Who is it?"

"Doug and Trevor,"

"Trevor's there?" he said, excited. "Is Camille there too?"

Jacob and Camille had been good friends who attended high school together in Gainesville. They had dated briefly and parted amicably. Jacob and Penelope met at Doug and Camille's wedding a little over five years before. And then Camille left Doug and basically cut all ties to family and friends. Jacob's opinion of Camille had been guarded ever since.

"No, she's not. But I'll let Doug will explain it to you," she said. "We'll be at Spanky's at seven. See you soon."

CHAPTER 12

THE LAST CHANCE Tavern was a drinking man's establishment. It was a one-story rectangular concrete block building put up in the early 1950s for the farming and citrus boom that never arrived. Over the decades the decor changed very little—dark paneled walls all around, a pool table, a dartboard, and a juke-box that might work if anyone would bother to plug it in. The bar itself lined one interior wall with booths along the opposite side. A few tables lay scattered along the center. There was no dance floor, but people did dance from time to time to music provided by a radio wired into a set of speakers fastened to the wall behind the bar. The station playing was chosen by whichever bartender had the early shift that day. The newest addition was a pair of 32" flat panel TVs hung at either end of the bar, tuned to either news or sports.

Penelope walked in the front door and had to stand for a few minutes for her eyes to adjust. The Last Chance patrons liked it dim inside. She went to the bar where she was ignored for a full minute—another Last Chance tradition. Finally, Terry O'Brien, the owner and bartender on duty, ambled over and stood in front of her, arms crossed, scowling.

"How's business, Terry?" Penelope asked.

Terry jerked his head backwards toward the six men spaced along the bar. "Good," he said.

"I need to ask you about last night. Was Doug Foster in here?"

"Yep." Terry turned and began to walk away.

"What time did he arrive?"

"Don't know," said Terry.

"Was he drunk when he got here?"

"Don't know," said Terry.

"Maybe you could tell me the names of some of the other people who were in here last night, so I can talk to them."

"Don't know," said Terry.

Penelope sighed. "Well, it looks like I'm going to have to call in some of the boys to hang out here all night tonight questioning your customers and staff. That won't be too disrupting on a Saturday night, will it?"

Terry turned around. "Look at the people in here, officer Chance. Every one of them is a bit drunk all of the time. Doug ain't no exception. My rule is if they can walk up to the bar and balance on a stool—they get served."

"So he didn't seem drunk when he arrived?"

"Nothing out of the ordinary, no."

"About what time did he get here?"

"Can't say for sure. I like to keep it casual. Don't make nobody clock in, you know." Penelope stared at him and he stared back. Finally, he said, "probably around eight."

"Thanks. You've been very helpful," Penelope said. "We probably won't have to come by tonight."

* * *

She went back to the station to add to her report and organize her thoughts. As soon as she got inside she saw a couple sitting at Jim Saunders' desk. Penelope immediately recognized them as Missy Clark's parents, Bob and Diane. They were agitated. Jim himself was looking pretty distressed as well.

"Thank the Lord you are here, Penny," Diane Clark exclaimed. "Make this man do something about our Missy. He is just not helping at all."

Penelope approached the couple and sat on the edge of her own neighboring desk. "Diane," she said. "I'm sure that officer Saunders is—"

"—not doing his job!" finished Bob Clark. "Or we would have our Missy back in our arms and that horrible man Tommy would be in jail!"

Penelope was determined to remain calm. "Officer Saunders, can you update me on the investigation please?"

Jim looked nervous. "Well, I found Missy's Facebook page."

"We forbid her to have one," interjected Diane. "We don't even have a computer in the house. We don't like the sort of things that go on the Internet."

Penelope stood and went behind Jim to look at his computer screen. "This is your daughter, Missy, isn't it?" she asked, indicating the smiling young woman whose face appeared on the screen in her Facebook profile.

Diane and Bob stared at the screen.

Diane gasped, "My baby! How could she do that? She doesn't have Internet. She doesn't have a phone..."

"He must have put her up to it," Bob said.

"There are computers at school," Penelope said. "And in the public library. Any clues as to where she might be?" Penelope asked Jim.

"Not really," he said. "Just a lot of typical teen stuff..."

Diane Clark moaned, "We should have home-schooled her so that she didn't have those negative influences," said Diane.

"...music, movies. Pictures of cats. No updates since Friday," Jim pointed out. "The last one was nothing but a heart. Several of her friends liked it."

Penelope peered over his shoulder. "Print out those names. We'll see if Mr. or Mrs. Clark recognizes any of them. What about Tommy's page?"

Jim switched to a different screen. "He likes motorcycles. Heavy metal music. Writes about trying to get into a film school in Orlando. In fact he says here that he's got big plans in Orlando this weekend."

"Go get him!" Diane exclaimed.

"That man has stolen money and taken our girl to Orlando to make a snuff film!" raged Bob.

Penelope tried not to roll her eyes. "Let's not get ahead of ourselves, Mr. and Mrs. Clark. First of all, do you recognize any of these friends?" She reached over Jim's shoulder to pick up the sheet of paper from his printer. Glancing at his computer screen, she noticed that there was a page open on the County Clerk's Office.

Jim Saunders saw Penelope notice the page. He appeared more uncomfortable than ever. He gave Penelope a questioning look.

She shook her head.

He immediately minimized the page.

Penelope handed the print-out to the Clarks.

"No!" Diane said, barely glancing at it. "We screen all of her friends. These people are not Missy's friends!"

"Mrs. Clark," Penelope tried to be tactful. "Teenagers naturally pull away from their parents a bit at this age. It looks like she may have had some friends and interests that you were not aware of."

"Our daughter is a good Christian. We did not raise her that way," Bob said angrily.

Diane began to cry. "That boy ruined her. We told

her she couldn't keep seeing him. I should have had him arrested the first time I saw him talking to Missy!"

Penelope said, "Mr. and Mrs. Clark. Tommy Pruett is just a few months older than your Missy. They are high-school sweethearts."

"Missy is not allowed to have a sweetheart," said Bob. "Especially not one like him!"

"He has a tattoo. He doesn't go to our church," said Diane.

"He doesn't go to any church," added Bob with disgust. "His family never has."

"That doesn't necessarily make him a bad person—" Jim Saunders began, but the look of astonishment on both of their faces cut him off.

Penelope sighed. The Pruett family was a boisterous bunch, living in the center of town. They operated the auto repair shop where Doug Foster worked. The family was loud and fun-loving and prone to having 'misunderstandings,' but no serious run-ins with the law. Tommy Pruett could, in Penelope's view, benefit from some spiritual guidance, but was still a decent young man. Two young people in love, one of them very sheltered and the other pretty much allowed to run free...opposites attract. "Mr. and Mrs. Clark, I am going to ask you to trust me. I will find your daughter. The best thing you can do is go home and pray."

"I'm not so sure that we can trust you, officer Chance," Bob Clark said. "Lately it seems that you have been protecting the wicked in our town."

"I take the side of the law..."

"And now you are taking the side of a drunken murderer!" Mr. Clark said.

"He's even living in your house!" Mrs. Clark said. "You claim to be a good Christian woman, but—"

"Mrs. Clark," Penelope said firmly. "I will thank you to leave my relationship with God between Him and myself. I have sworn do my duty to protect the innocent and bring the guilty to justice according to the laws of the United States, Florida and our county, in that order. As for God's laws, I do my best to follow them as well, and I leave Him to make His own judgment. Now please, go home and let us work. I will contact you as soon as I know anything about Missy's whereabouts."

Mr. and Mrs. Clark turned and left without another word.

As soon as they were gone Jim said, "Whoooeee. I thought there was going to be lightning shooting out of your eyes for a minute there!"

"They're good people. They're just worried about their daughter."

Jim maximized the County Clerk Office page. It showed that three days before, a Thomas Justin Pruett and a Missy Rose Clark had applied for a marriage license. In Florida, a person over the age of sixteen does not need parental consent.

"And you chose not to tell them about this..." Jim

said.

Penelope's conscience bothered her about that. She hated to lie and withholding information was indeed a form of lying. "Well, if the deed is done, it's done," she justified. "It's a family issue now—nothing to do with the law. Keep the BOLO going for Tommy's car. We still need to talk to them about the missing money. Two hundred dollars isn't going to get them very far."

"Will do," said Jim.

Penelope sat at her own desk and rubbed her temples. "Dear Lord," she prayed silently. "Help me to remember that You work in mysterious ways. When I complained to You a few days ago about this town being too quiet I didn't quite expect You to answer with challenges as big as these. I know You would never give me anything I can't handle...and I will try to appreciate and live up to the confidence that You have in me."

She raised her head and noticed Jim staring at her from the corner of his eye. Penelope was never ashamed of expressing her faith in public but it was sometimes a cause of curiosity or even amusement to those around her who didn't feel it as deeply as she did. She smiled at him. He turned back to his computer screen.

CHAPTER 13

INSIDE SPANKY'S GRILL, the local family restaurant, Trevor sat in a booster seat at their table, stuffing chicken nuggets into his mouth.

Jacob had met them in the parking lot. Penelope embraced him tightly and he whispered into her ear that he loved to see her in her uniform, but wasn't she supposed to be off duty?

She gave him a brief version of the day's events as she removed her weapon and utility belt, stowing them in the lock box in the truck of her cruiser. He nodded once and left it at that. He had to be the most understanding man in the world. Doug watched their affectionate display with a mixed expression of jealousy and sadness. Penelope now had the very thing Doug had thought he'd found with Camille.

Inside the restaurant, Jacob watched Trevor eat. He laughed. "My goodness, Doug, he's getting so big he'll be wearing his daddy's clothes before long."

Trevor laughed and said, "You're silly, Uncle Jay-Jay."

He smiled to hear the boy's pet name for him. "You haven't called me that in a long time. You sure have a good memory for a five year old."

"Mama said we might come back now. That's what daddy said." He stuffed another nugget in his cheek and sipped soda through his straw.

Jacob exchanged a look with Penelope. He knew, just like Penelope did, how badly Doug wanted his family back together again. He leaned over and tickled Trevor's ribs to break the sudden tension. Trevor laughed and spilled soda down his chin.

"Daddy!" he complained. "He tickled me!"

"He did?" Doug asked in mock surprise. "What do you think I should do about that? Call the cops?"

"Penny's a cop!" shouted Trevor.

Everyone at the table broke out in laughter.

It felt good to Penelope to have the three of them together. It was like things were the way they had been, back before Doug's divorce. Back before all the troubles they were facing that day started happening.

Several other couples and groups and single people were in Spanky's. And a lot of those people cast a lot of glances their way, all directed at Doug. Whispered conversations followed those looks. Penelope was reminded that no matter how good this moment felt, there was still a cloud of suspicion hanging over her friend's head.

Jacob saw it too, and squeezed her hand. "You'll figure it out," he said to her. "I have faith in you."

"Me too, Penny," Doug said, ruffling his son's hair. "I know you'll make everyone see I didn't do this."

"Do what?" Trevor asked in an innocent little boy's voice.

"Steal all the french fries in town," Doug told him, picking one off his son's plate and popping it into his mouth.

"Hey!" Trevor cried out, grabbing for the fry too late. "Daddy!"

Doug winked at Penelope and she saw the confidence that Jacob and Doug had in her. She hoped she would live up to their expectations. And her own.

The rest of their meal went quickly and they were soon headed back to Penelope's place. Jacob said goodbye to her with a hug and a kiss.

Back in her own home, Penelope turned the television on for Trevor and set it to one of the cartoon channels. The boy sat down happily on the floor with his trucks and his stuffed dog and stared at a big, goofy looking bear trying to eat a bag of pretzels. He'd be happy for hours.

"Doug, I'm going to take a shower. Why don't you try to call Camille?" she said over her shoulder as she headed for her room and a change of clothes.

She took longer in the shower than she had intended. The hot water just felt so good on her tired muscles. When she came back out toweling her hair dry in her PJs and robe, she found Doug in the living room floor with Trevor playing an elaborate game of race cars involving a track built out of books from Penelope's bookshelf. She smiled and hoped she and Jacob would be doing something just like that with their own son one day.

"Did you get a hold of Camille?" she asked Doug.

Her friend shook his head, racing his car next to Trevor's and not looking up. "Tried. Still no answer. Beep beep!" he said to Trevor, passing his car.

"Hey!" Trevor said, and sped his own car up to pass his dad's again.

Doug was a great dad to his son. There had to be something more to this attempted murder case that Doug was caught up in.

There had to be! She just wasn't seeing it.

CHAPTER 14

AFTER DOUG PUT his son to sleep in the spare bedroom, Penelope waited for him to come back out into the living room. She sipped at a cup of coffee and tried to fit together mis-matched puzzle pieces. She turned every piece of information she knew every way she could think to turn it. Nothing seemed to fit.

Doug flopped down next to her on the couch. "I can't believe Trevor's back, you know, Penny? I haven't wanted a beer all day. I'd almost given up hope. That's why I kept hitting the drink so hard. I mean, losing Camille was bad enough, but losing Trevor was the hardest. The worst. "

"God never gives us more than we can handle," Penelope said to him. "I honestly believe that, Doug."

Her friend nodded. He wasn't convinced. "So, I guess I failed his test? I mean, God threw all this at me and all

I could do was drink myself into oblivion every night."
He looked at Penelope with the expression of a man
accustomed to being looked down on.

"I'm not going to judge you, Doug. You dealt with
things in your own way. If you think it wasn't the right
way, then you're free to do something about that, right?"

"Yeah," Doug said, hesitating. "Things that are done...
they can't be undone."

Penelope heard something in her friend's words.
"Doug, is there something you need to tell me?"

He put his head down into his hands, raking his
fingers through his hair. "I didn't tell you the whole
reason that Camille was here."

Not what Penelope had expected him to say, but it
was better than the confession she had braced herself for.

Able to breathe again, she said, "I was wondering
about that. I was happy to hear she came back, but it just
didn't seem like I was getting the whole story."

"You weren't, Penny, you weren't, but I couldn't talk
about it in front of Trevor, you know?"

Penelope waited. When Doug didn't say anything
more for more than a minute, she prompted, "You can
tell me, Doug. I've always been here for you, right?"

Doug managed a small smile. "Yeah, you have. You've
been like a sister to me, Penny. All this time after Camille
left me, you've been there for me. Everyone else in town
wrote me off. But you've always been there for me."

"So let me be there for you now. What did Camille

tell you?"

Doug took a deep breath and let it out slowly. "She told me something about her new boyfriend. The...uh... guy she took up with after she left me. The one she's been living with, with my Trevor."

The heat in his voice was hard to miss.

"She said that she had started to think, maybe this guy isn't who he said he was. Maybe this guy's something way worse."

"Like...what?"

Doug looked at her for a moment, but then his face shut down. "That's it," he said. "He's just not who she thought he was." He stood up.

"That's not all she said, Doug..."

He began walking toward the stairs. "You know, Penny, it's been a real long day."

"You can talk to me, Doug. You need to talk to me."

"I'm gonna jump in the shower," he said, taking the stairs two at a time, obviously wanting to avoid the conversation.

Penny watched him go, feeling frustrated and helpless. *Please God, help me help this man. Guide me with Your wisdom to lead him to peace...and justice, if it comes to that.*

She really hoped it wouldn't come to that. Penelope shook her head. Whatever information Doug had would wait, she supposed. Her friend had earned some sleep. If Penelope's past few days had been rough, Doug's had been ten times worse. Penelope wasn't the one accused of trying to run down a friend with a very distinctive truck.

But, why? How did any of this make any sense? Where was the motive? It wasn't simply a matter of intoxication. Everything she'd learned so far told her that Doug probably wasn't drunk before he got to The Last Chance Tavern. Not drunk enough anyway for an accomplished drunk like Doug. It took a lot to get to the point where the alcohol clouded his memory.

Penelope took her cell phone and slipped outside onto the front porch. She dialed the number of the one person she knew she could talk to.

"Hello, officer beautiful," Jacob said to her in a slightly tired voice.

"Hi sweetheart," she said, a smile slipping onto her face. "I know we just saw each other a little while ago, but I needed to hear a friendly voice."

"And I was the first person you thought of?" he joked.

"Yeah," she said simply, too worn out to joke back.

"This whole mess is really weighing you down, isn't it?"

"I just feel like I'm failing him. Doug, I mean. I feel there is something more I should be doing, something I should be seeing that I'm missing."

Jacob was quiet for a long time before he said anything else. "Penny, I'm going to suggest something to you, but I don't want you to get upset with me," he said.

"I won't" she said, unconvincingly. She knew she

didn't want to hear it.

He sighed deeply through the phone. "Has it occurred to you that over the years maybe Doug has learned how to make you believe him even though he's not telling the truth? That maybe, just maybe, he's learned to lie to you?"

She pulled the phone away from her ear as if it would help her unhear what he had just said. She took a deep breath, pacing, before she brought the phone back up.

"No," was her simple response. There had been a little more heat in it than she had intended.

He sounded apologetic as he said, "I'm sorry, Penny. The last thing I want is for you to be upset with me, but it had to be said."

"I'm not upset with you for saying it," she said. "You're right. I mean, I wouldn't be doing my job if I didn't at least consider it."

"I'm sorry, Penny," he said. "I know how close you two are. I know how hard it was for you, growing up."

"Other than you," Penelope said, her voice beginning to quaver, "he's all I have. After what happened, you know..." A tear escaped the corner of her eye and spilled down her cheek. "I can't give up on him. I have to believe in him."

"And that is why I love you, Penny. I am so grateful to God for bringing a woman like you to me to complete my life. When you are in pain, so am I. I don't want this to be true, Penny. But if it is, then we need to find out. I'll help you. I'll stand by you. I promise."

"God truly blessed me when He brought us together. I love you so much, Jacob." She thanked God silently for his strength as she ran a hand through her hair. Then, defiantly, she said, "I don't have to believe it until it's the only thing left. Until then, I'm going to do my best to get this mess figured out."

"And if it comes down to Doug lying to you as the only thing left, what then?"

"I'll deal with it if and when it gets to that point," Penelope replied. "Dear God, I hope it doesn't come to that."

"Amen," Jacob said.

"I love you," she said to him.

"I love you back," he answered. It was their special little code.

After the call ended, Penelope decided to go to bed. It had been a long day and the next day would probably be another long one.

Dear Lord, she prayed, *please help me to handle all the work You've set before me. I can only do this with You at my side. Amen.*

It wasn't long before she was sound asleep, dreaming nightmares of another time, of another wound that wouldn't heal, of a two-story house that used to stand in what was now an empty lot just before the Southside Bridge, not far from The Last Chance Tavern.

CHAPTER 15

EARLY SUNDAY MORNING, way too early, Penelope awoke to the bouncing of a small body on her bed and Trevor's high-pitched young voice.

"Auntie Penny waked up!" Trevor shouted in her face. She must have been crazy to hope for kids early in her marriage with Jacob.

Then Trevor hugged her around her neck, and she knew she'd be willing to lose any amount of sleep to have this every morning.

"Good morning, little buddy," Penelope said cheerfully as she grabbed the boy in a bear hug.

Trevor squirmed in Penelope's grip, squealing and laughing. Penelope kissed the top of the boy's light blond head and released him. Trevor had his mother's hair and his father's piercing blue eyes, a combination that Penelope thought was stunning, especially for a boy.

Watching Trevor run around her bedroom, Penelope said, "Why don't you go wake up your dad so that I can get dressed and get ready? Then, after we eat some breakfast, we'll play in the back yard for a little while."

As long as work doesn't call me again, she thought.

Trevor stopped and looked at Penelope with his head tilted to one side, regarding Penelope with as much seriousness as a five year old could manage.

"Auntie Penny, when is mama coming?"

Penelope cleared whatever cobwebs had been left in her mind to give Trevor her full attention. "I don't know, buddy. We tried calling her last night but she must have been real busy. What did she say to you when she dropped you off here?"

"She jus' said, Stay with your daddy and be good."

And before Penelope could say anything else Trevor ran off shouting to his dad that it was time to wake up, Auntie Penny said so.

Penelope rolled out of bed, feeling as though she'd been pushing a Mack truck uphill. Most Sundays she went to the mid-morning contemporary service at her church, but she didn't think it was a good idea to invite Doug and Trevor, given their current situation. Maybe once this whole thing blew over—there was a wonderful children's program and the church also offered substance-abuse counseling. Penny sighed, knowing that she was getting ahead of herself. She put on jeans, sneakers and a t-shirt and made her way down to the kitchen to get some cereal and coffee.

She found Doug already there, munching Fruity Bits cereal right next to his little boy. "Morning Doug," Penelope said. "How'd you sleep?"

"About as well as you could expect with a wiggle-worm kicking me in the side all night," he grinned and tousled his son's hair. "I'm looking forward to getting back home. I'll have to update Trevor's room—it's still got his baby stuff in it."

"I'm not a baby!" Trevor protested.

"No, you sure aren't," his dad agreed.

"Have you tried calling Camille this morning?"

"Yep," said Doug. "No answer."

"We need to finish our talk from last night," Penelope started to say.

"Later, Penelope, okay? When Trevor goes down for his nap. Okay?" His voice pleaded with his friend.

And Penelope relented. "Okay. But then we talk, right?"

With a fresh cup of coffee in hand, Penelope took out the box of instant oatmeal just in time to have the phone ring. 'Police Station' flashed on the caller display.

Of course, Penelope thought.

Answering, she said, "officer Chance."

It was Jim Saunders on the other end of the phone once more. "Osceola County Sheriff's department spotted Tommy's car pulling out of a parking lot at a low-rent motel down on 192 in Kissimmee. Do you want me to have them pick them up?"

Penelope considered this. "No," she said, finally. "Let's give them the chance to do the right thing and come on home."

"What about the money they stole?"

"Allegedly," said Penny. "Let's give them the chance to come clean about it. Keep an eye out for his car coming back into town and pull them over then. No sense involving other counties if we don't have to."

"Alright," said Jim. "There's only the two ways into Franklin. Not hard to watch both. If we have the manpower, that is..."

Penelope sighed. Here goes her Sunday, she thought. "What's the problem?"

"Well, you know Chief Jackson is down in Clermont visiting his grandma. Peterson's wife and daughters all have the flu and he needs to stay home and take care of them. And your boys DeBose and Walker never did come back from their stolen car investigation in Gainesville last night."

"We have two missing officers?"

"Well, not exactly missing," drawled Jim. "They were scheduled off today anyway and I think they were going to hang out for the music festival over there last night."

"You think?"

"They told me they were going to hang out for the music festival last night. So that means today we got three out of town, one out sick. Someone has to mind the station and that would be Marty Reardon. That leaves just me on patrol...Hopefully we'll have a quiet day."

Penelope sighed heavily through her nose. Hopefully they would. After a moment she said, "Okay, let's do it like this. The kids won't be back for at least two hours and that's if they don't stop along the way. You take the east end of Main and have Marty lock up the station and take the west end. When one of you picks them up take them back to the station and I'll meet you there."

"Sounds like a plan," Jim said. "Thanks Penelope."

"Yeah, sure," she said. "You really owe me lunch now. I'd sure like to know what got into their heads to make them do something like this."

"I guess Missy is a good girl like you, but she was in a hurry and didn't want to bother with a long engagement," Jim said. Penelope could hear the smirk in his voice. She ignored it.

"Oh, I forgot to tell you what DeBose and Walker came up with in Gainesville. They nabbed ole Brother George Flannagan out there."

"So it wasn't just a frat boy thing?"

"It started out like that, but sometimes they brought in nice cars. Those they were sellin' to a chop shop."

"Oh, wow," Penelope replied. "What about the cars from Franklin?"

"They were still there, undamaged. Gainesville PD promised to return them to us right after they're processed."

"Great," Penelope said. "Thanks for letting me know, Jim. You're right. Good news for a change."

"Sure thing," Jim replied. "Figured you could use some. Uh. How's the thing with Doug going?"

Penelope chose her words carefully, walking down the hallway nearer to the bedrooms, farther from the kitchen where Doug and Trevor sat, before she answered. "I'm not sure anymore. There's something else going on here, Jim. Doug has something to tell me about his ex-wife. I know it's something important but he doesn't want to talk in front of his kid."

"Smart," Jim said. "Too many parents put this stuff on their kids."

"Yeah. I'm sure that's all it is. Still, there's way too many puzzle pieces that fit outside the borders on this one, you know what I mean?"

"Sure do," said Jim. "Alright. I'll update Marty on the plan for today. Take some time with your company, Penelope."

"Thanks, Jim." She walked back into the kitchen and saw Doug had already taken Trevor out to the back yard. On a hunch, Penelope dialed Camille's number once more. Still no answer. She sighed and then went outside to join in a game of catch.

A little over two hours later, she got the call.

CHAPTER 16

WHEN PENELOPE ENTERED the police station, she found Missy and Tommy each occupying one of the two holding pens.

"Did they give you any trouble?" she asked Jim Saunders. He was leaning back in his chair with his feet on his desk, trying to act like an old-school scary sheriff.

"Not too much," he drawled. "The boy's a bit lippy though..."

"Officer Chance," Tommy said. "I'm not sure what we're doing here."

"Seems to have got over it..." Jim commented.

"Did you give him a list of charges?" Penelope asked.

"Yep. The eight-one-two-point-oh-one-for-five, a eight-one-two-point-one-three, and a seven-eight-seven-point-oh-one."

"Oh, a seven-eight-seven-point-oh-one," Penelope said. "That's going to be problematic."

"We didn't do anything wrong!" Missy cried.

"You put a scare into your parents, for starters," Penelope replied. "They reported you as missing yesterday afternoon."

Missy said defiantly, "We're married now. That means I'm an adult now in the eyes of the law. I don't have to report to them anymore."

"You're absolutely correct, Missy," Penelope said. "Unless they petition the court to have your marriage annulled."

Missy seemed shocked. "They can do that?"

"Yes, they can," Penelope told her. "You were a minor when you left home with Tommy here, and under their responsibility. They want him charged with kidnapping."

"That's bull!" Tommy shouted.

"He's my husband," Missy declared.

Penelope crossed her arms and regarded them. "Have the two of you really thought this out? Last I checked, Missy, you still live with your parents and you're still in high school. Now that you've come home where do you think you're going to live?"

Tommy and Missy glanced at each other.

"We can live with my parents," Tommy said. "I work at the shop and I'm saving money. I know motorcycle repair and I'm going to get a better job in Orlando."

"You really think it's that easy," Jim chuckled.

"Why not?" asked Tommy. His innocence was genuine.

Missy was sincere. "We were always going to get married some day. We've been in love for a long time."

Penelope looked at her. "So why not tell your parents about it?"

"They hate me!" exclaimed Tommy.

"They do," agreed Missy.

"And you thought this would be the best way to solve that problem?" Jim asked.

"Missy, your parents care about you very much. You should have talked to them."

Missy began to cry. "I can't talk to them, officer Chance. They won't listen. All they do is talk about how much I disappoint them and God with my behavior!"

Penelope chose her words carefully. "They think it's important for you to follow a Christian way of life..."

"This is no life!" Missy cried. "They wouldn't let me listen to music or read a book that wasn't about God! They wouldn't let me go online! They wouldn't let me have a phone..."

"The world is a rough place," Penelope told her. "They wanted to protect you from outside influences."

"Evil influences like me?" Tommy asked.

"I didn't say that..."

"No, but they did," Tommy said. "Officer Chance, you know I'm not evil. I never did anything wrong. Just because I don't go to church don't make me an evil person."

Penelope said, "You're right..."

"He's smart, too," said Missy. "He got accepted to film school. Now that we're going to be a family he can get financial aid."

"A family?" Penelope inquired. Now the truth was revealed.

Tommy and Missy had let their teenage desires get the better of them and Missy was pregnant.

"It was just the one time," Missy said with tears in her eyes. "We prayed about it and asked for forgiveness and promised God that we wouldn't do it again before we were married—"

"But it was too late," Tommy said. "So I did the right thing. We got married."

Penelope knew their logic was a little backward, but considering the position they had put themselves in, she kind of had to admire them for the way they had tried to work it out. God works in mysterious ways, indeed.

She sighed. "Okay, you both need to tell your parents what you just told me, and the sooner, the better. They won't like it, but as you said, you're adults now. And like I said, you need to start acting like adults."

"We were going to tell mom and dad when we got back," Missy said. "Maybe you can come with us?" she asked hopefully.

"No," Penelope said. "This is something you need to do as an adult."

The teenagers looked at each other for a few moments and then nodded. "Okay, officer," Missy said.

"Are you going to let us out now?" Tommy asked.

Penelope had almost forgotten the main reason the pair was locked up. "There's another matter I need to speak to you about. Missy, Mr. Dobson says your register was two hundred dollars short Friday night."

"Yes, it was," Missy replied, a look of surprise on her face. "That's because I cashed a check for Mrs. Jamison. Mr. Dobson does it all of the time. Oh, my gosh...I think I left her check under the cash drawer! I can't believe he would think I stole from him! Can I call him right now and tell him about it?"

"We'll give him a call and check up on your story," Penelope said. That sounded more like the Missy she knew. "I'm glad to find out this was just a misunderstanding."

"Thank you," Missy said. "I really need this job...now more than ever."

"I suppose you do," Penelope agreed.

Jim had been standing nearby during the entire conversation and Penelope looked over at him. "Are you satisfied enough to let the kids go home now? It's your case."

"Sure, I'm good with it," Jim replied. To Missy and Tommy he said, "I'm gonna call your parents and let them know you'll be home soon. So I expect you're gonna do just that, right?" He unlocked Missy first and then Tommy.

"Yes sir, officer," Tommy said. Addressing Penelope, he added, "And thank you too, ma'am. I promise you that we take this seriously. We'll prove ourselves to you. Wait and see."

"Couldn't ask for more than that," Penelope told him sincerely. "If either of you ever need to talk to someone about anything, I'm here for you."

"Yes, ma'am," Tommy said. "We'll remember that."

The newlyweds rose from their seats and walked out of the Police station, hand in hand.

"I sure hope that check is where Missy says it is," Jim said.

Penelope turned to Jim and said, "It will be."

Jim smiled at her. "You don't think that sometimes you're too trusting?"

"I go with my gut," she said. "And it is reminding me right now that you owe me lunch."

Jim nodded. "Sure enough. Deal's a deal. You got anythin' in mind?"

"As a matter of fact, I do."

CHAPTER 17

PENELOPE RETURNED HOME with a large pizza from The Pizza Palace containing a stuffed crust with pepperoni and mushrooms. One half had anchovies on it. She'd come to accept that she was fairly unique in her love for anchovies. Except for Jacob. Their first date had been over pepperoni and anchovy pizza. She had known then, that very night, that the two of them would be together, and that God had sent her someone special.

Doug was waiting for her in the kitchen, downing another cup of coffee.

"You could just start mainlining that stuff, you know," Penelope said to her friend as she set the box down on the kitchen table.

"Would you prefer I drink beer?" he asked?

"Good point," Penelope conceded.

The pizza box was big enough to take up most of her tiny table's space. Penelope would have to upgrade her furniture when she and Jacob finally got married. It was all basic stuff she wasn't attached to anyway, not like she owned any family heirlooms. That thought sent her into a momentary flashback and she was suddenly sad.

Doug opened the pizza box and made a face. "Anchovies? Really?"

Penelope snapped out of it and laughed. "It's good to have you back to your old self, Doug. Even just a little. Having Trevor here has been good for you. Where is the little guy?"

"Napping," Doug said, taking a slice out of the box from the non-anchovy side and starting in on it without waiting for Penelope to produce plates.

Penelope sat down opposite her friend and took a slice of her own. "Good. Then let's talk about Camille."

For just a minute Doug's eyes opened wider and his pizza seemed to get stuck in his craw. "What do you mean?"

Penelope chewed slowly. "Any word from her yet?"

"No," he said.

"So, last night you started to explain to me what she had told you about her current boyfriend."

Doug nodded. "Right. That." He brushed crumbs from his hands. "Well. See. The guy's name is Michael Findley. He's real sketchy. I knew that. I met him once, just by accident, but it was enough. So, anyway. That's why Camille brought Trevor to me, Penelope. To keep him safe."

"Is that what she said?"

Doug looked down at his hands, at the clock, at the pizza, everywhere except at Penelope. "I don't know what to do, Penny. I don't know what I can do, seeing how I'm on house arrest under suspicion of trying to kill one of my friends."

Penelope said, leaning forward, her elbows on the table, "What did Camille tell you? What exactly did she say?"

"It's not what she said, it's how she acted. She's scared."

"You think she might be in real trouble? You're telling me this now, now, after we haven't been able to reach Camille for over twenty-four hours?"

"I'm the town drunk that tried to kill the other town drunk, Penny. Now I'm saying that my ex-wife's boyfriend isn't a nice man. How does that sound?"

"You were supposed to trust me, Doug!" Penelope realized her voice was getting louder, but she just didn't care. She had been working straight out for the last few days, and had been trying her best to keep Doug from being arrested for attempted murder on top of everything else, and now it turned out Doug was keeping secrets from her.

It was just too much.

"I know, Penny, I know," Doug said to her, raising

a hand to his forehead. "I thought Camille could work things out. She's a tough woman, you know that. If she took up with a scum-bag, then that's kind of all on her. As long as Trevor is safe...and he is."

"So you were going to leave Camille to deal with a man she's afraid of on her own just so that you could keep your son?" Penny was incredulous.

Doug stared at her for a moment and then shook his head. "Well, it sounds bad when you put it that way. And I know that. That's why I'm telling you now. I'm sorry. I thought if you knew everything, then you'd hold it against me, too."

The house phone rang.

Penelope yanked the receiver off its cradle on the second ring.

"Officer Chance!" she snapped.

Silence for a few seconds, and then Jim's hesitant voice. "Penelope? You okay?"

Penelope forced herself to take a breath before answering, and to lower her tone. "No, Jim. I'm not okay. But, just...don't worry about that. What are you calling for?"

"Uh, well, I'm thinkin' you should come back in for this one."

Trevor toddled out from the hallway that led to the bedrooms, rubbing his eyes.

Doug went over and picked up his little boy.

"Listen, Jim, I'm kind of in the middle of something

here. Whatever it is, can you get one of the other guys to help you out with it?"

"I'm afraid I can't, Penelope. Kind of directly involves you. And Doug. You should bring him in with you."

That last bit got her attention. "What is it, Jim?"

"We just got a report in from Gainesville," Jim told her. "Report is on a deceased female they found this morning. Single gunshot to the back of her head."

Penelope's mind put it together before Jim could finish. "Oh, please God, no," she said.

Penelope could hear Jim draw a breath even through the phone line. "I'm afraid that's the way of it, Penelope. Camille Foster. She's dead. Sometime in the last thirty-six hours, is the preliminary."

Penelope nodded and swallowed back a sudden lump in her throat. "I understand, Jim. You did the right thing, calling me. I'll be in soon. Did you call the Chief yet?"

"Yup. First call. You were my second."

"Thanks, Jim."

Hanging up the phone, she turned to see Doug stuffing a paper towel down the front of Trevor's shirt and giving him a slice of pizza. How did you tell your best friend that his ex-wife was dead? How did you tell him she was murdered? Worse, how did you tell his little boy?

"Doug," she started, figuring God would give her the words as she went along. "I, uh, have something to tell you. Why don't we let Trevor eat by himself for a minute?"

"I know, Penny," Doug interrupted her.

Penelope felt a chill. "You know what?" she asked cautiously.

"About Camille." He looked at her over Trevor's head. "I guess they found her then."

CHAPTER 18

WHY DID GOD allow bad things to happen to good people?

Penelope pondered that question a lot on Sunday afternoon as she sat in the Police station with her best friend sitting on the opposite side of a two-way mirror, waiting to be questioned like a criminal.

Might as well ask Him why He put mosquitoes on Earth, Penelope finally decided. Both of those questions had just about the same answer. He has a plan that the human mind can't begin to comprehend.

"The Chief's on his way?" Penelope asked Jim again.

Jim nodded, running a knuckle over his handlebar mustache. "He's on his way back from Clermont. Will be here in an hour or so." Jim's thick southern accent had always kind of amused Penelope.

Not today. Nothing was funny today. Penelope had

gone out of her way for Doug in this, put her personal reputation out on a limb, even putting her own career in jeopardy, to stick up for Doug. And Doug had repaid her by lying to her.

"You sure you wanna take this one, Penelope?" Jim asked her.

"Chief Jackson asked me to handle this case. Even if Doug is my friend." She pulled her hair back into a ponytail, and sighed. "Okay. I'm going to start. Make sure the camera's on for me, all right?"

After Jim nodded, Penelope stepped through the metal door and into the interview room. She had a notepad and pen in hand as she sat down across from Doug. The two friends looked at each other silently for a long moment.

"I didn't kill my wife, Penny," Doug said finally.

"Ex-wife," Penelope corrected him.

Her friend shrugged his shoulders. "I don't see how that matters now. Do you?"

"Everything matters in a murder investigation, Doug." Penelope clicked the nib of the pen out and placed it on the table next to the pad of paper.

Doug looked down at his hands resting on top of the metal interview table and didn't reply.

"Okay, Doug," Penelope said. "You and I are going to talk to each other now. We're going to talk, and I'm going to talk to you like a police officer. Tell me how you knew that Camille was dead."

Doug opened his mouth to speak and then closed it again.

"Fine, Doug. Fine. You have the right to remain silent."

"Penny, come on."

"You have the right to talk to a lawyer before answering any of my questions. If you cannot afford to hire a lawyer—"

"Penny, seriously—"

"—one will be appointed to you—"

"—you don't need to do this!"

"—without cost to you—"

"Penny!"

"—without cost and before—"

"Penny! Stop it! Okay, okay. Camille talked to me for just a few minutes when she dropped off Trevor yesterday. She told me about her boyfriend, told me I had to keep Trevor because he wasn't safe with her, and then she left. Just took off. After two years of no contact with me at all, she just dumps Trevor with me and leaves."

Penelope scratched out some notes. "You already told me that. I'm asking you how you knew she was dead?"

"Because..." He stopped, took several breaths, and Penelope thought he was going to clam up again, but finally he spoke. "Because I went over to Gainesville to find her. I was worried. I went to her apartment."

"When?"

"Last night after we all went to bed. I borrowed your

car and went to her apartment."

Penelope stared at him. "You took my car without asking and left Trevor alone?"

Her friend scrubbed his face. He still couldn't believe he'd done that, either. "I know, I know. It was stupid. I wasn't thinking straight."

"You think?" Penelope couldn't keep the sarcasm out of her voice. "You were supposed to stay at my house, Doug. That was the whole point of me bringing you there, to keep suspicion off you, and help you clear your name. You think this helps you clear your name?"

"That's why I didn't tell you about it right off."

"You didn't tell me about it at all."

"I was trying to, Penny. I was talking to you about it when this happened."

"So, bad timing." Sarcasm again.

Doug just shook his head and looked down at the table.

"So tell me now. What happened when you stole my car, abandoned your five-year old son and left Franklin against my direct say-so?"

Doug winced as though he had been stung by Penelope's words. Their friendship meant a lot to both of them, and this was bringing it to its breaking point.

"I was worried about her. You know we couldn't get her on the phone. So I went to her apartment," Doug confessed. "Same one that she's had since she left me. I went upstairs, went to her door, and I called her name.

She didn't answer and I got mad. I yelled through the door. I told her I needed to talk to her and warned her not to run away from me again. I was yelling at her, and all the anger I had for her was just coming out of me, and then I punched the door. It swung right open and then I saw her, Penny. I saw her on the floor. Dead. Blood, her blood, making a puddle behind her head."

Doug broke down into tears. Penelope let him cry it out for a few seconds. She had to think like a cop now, not a friend. "I'm sorry, Doug. I really am. But we have to go on. So when the report from Camille's neighbors says that they heard you having an argument with her, that was you yelling from outside before you found her dead?"

Her friend shook his head.

"Doug, look, whatever's going on here, I need to know. Lay it all out for me, please. Lay it at God's feet. The truth sets you free. You know that."

Doug raised his head and looked at her and then with an expression that came close to contempt asked, "Oh, really? Is that what it's done for you? The truth set you free, did it, Penny?"

Penelope was stunned into silence for almost a minute. Doug was referring to something from deep in Penelope's past. A horrible incident that had left a family decimated and Penelope's childhood home burned to the ground. And Doug was right—Penelope hadn't dealt with that issue yet. It still haunted her. The house, in flames, and Penelope at a very young age screaming for help...

She shook the images out of her mind and concentrated on the here and now. "I'm trying to help you right now, Doug," Penelope finally said. "Right now your present is my only concern. What happened to Camille, Doug?"

Doug sniffed back his tears and shrugged again. "I don't know."

"Doug, come on now."

"I don't know, I tell you! When I got there, she was dead."

"So you just left. You didn't think to call the police?"

"I couldn't stick around—Trevor was back home asleep without me! I couldn't help her and I knew what people would think. If I had called the police and then waited for them I'd be arrested and in a jail in Gainesville right now, farther from my boy."

Penelope had known that something was wrong with her friend. She could sense the change in him as soon as she came home Saturday and Doug had told him Camille had come back. That Trevor had come back. Penelope had chalked it up to the presence of Doug's son in his life again. She hadn't wanted to believe that Doug would ever try to hide something from her.

But it hadn't taken her long to realize Doug was doing exactly that. For the first time ever, she had thought Doug might be lying to her. Doug had never lied to her before. Until now. And Penelope had seen it happening, but had not wanted to believe it. Even Jacob had suggested the possibility to her, and she had turned a blind eye to the very thought.

She had put away both her police officer intuition and her God-given reason because she hadn't wanted to believe what was right in front of her eyes.

God help me, she thought. *Give me strength. Please.*

"So you knew she was dead all morning?" she said to Doug, as a statement, not a question.

Doug nodded his head, miserably.

"Even when I was trying to call her to talk to her?"

Another nod.

"Doug. Did you kill Camille?"

"No!" Doug said immediately.

"I want to believe you, Doug. If there is anything else you aren't telling me it's about time right now.

Slowly, Doug reached into the back pocket of his jeans and pulled out a folded and crumpled piece of paper.

CHAPTER 19

PENELOPE READ OVER that paper three times.

It was a wanted poster from the state of California. There was a photograph and basic information describing a man by the name of Michael Findley, height five-foot-eleven, weight two-hundred and ten, black hair and hazel eyes. Snake tattoo on the back of his right hand and barbed wire tattoo circling his left bicep. Wanted for armed robbery. And according to Doug, the man in the photo was Camille's current boyfriend.

The poster listed, among other things, that Findley was wanted for questioning in a murder case. Had Camille found this out and confronted Findley? Had he killed her to keep her quiet? Or had they argued and he pushed her, or...or...or. Too many possibilities.

But one thing was for sure: without the wanted

Mr. Findley in hand, the only person on the hook for Camille's murder was Doug.

Everything pointed to Doug. No matter how much Penelope believed in him, the evidence all pointed squarely at Doug.

Please God, Penelope prayed after locking Doug in the holding cell and sitting down at her desk once again. *Let me figure a way out of this for Doug. He's not a perfect man, Lord, but he's my friend. And if he's innocent, he doesn't deserve this.*

If? If he's innocent? Penelope heard the way she had said it and wondered at herself. Was she beginning to think Doug was guilty too?

Penelope had stayed at her desk through the afternoon, doing paperwork and waiting for the chief to arrive. It was going to be necessary to charge Doug, in the absence of any proof that might show his innocence. Oh, she had a few details that tended to bolster Doug's story of where he had been on the day Pete got run down, but nothing concrete. And nothing that she could present to a jury as an alibi. Finding that proof would have to be her next step.

Actually, her next step would be to call Jacob. He had agreed to take care of Trevor and she wanted to check on both of them. She loved that little boy almost as if he was her own. But more than that, she needed to hear some encouraging words from the most important man in her life.

She was just about to press the speed dial to call him when his face popped up on the screen. He was calling her. She smiled—they were truly a couple in sync with each other. "Hi sweetheart," she said cheerfully when she accepted the call.

"Hi, honey," he answered and instantly she knew something was wrong.

"What is it? Did you hear bad news about Pete?"

"No. In fact, he's cleared to go home when he wants."

Penelope closed her eyes and exhaled with relief. "Thank you, Lord," she said.

"Penny, I took Trevor out to the grocery store and we spent some time in the park. Someone was in my house while we were gone."

That set off every one of Penelope's alarm bells. "Who was it?" she asked.

"I wish I knew, Penny," he said. "As soon as I walked back into the house I felt as if something was out of place, but I didn't know what. You know that feeling you get when there's something you're so familiar with that you just never think about it, but then it's changed, you can't put your finger on it? Well, it was like that. So I started looking around the house and I finally figured it out. Remember that big photograph up on the living room wall of me, you, Doug and Camille. It's gone."

"Just that picture?" she asked him, while asking herself who steals just a framed photo.

"Just that, Penny. I can't see anything else missing."

"Jacob, I want you to get out of that house..."

"We are," he said. "I took Trevor back to the park."

"Good thinking. How long were you out of the house?"

"Maybe two hours, tops."

"And you're sure that was all that was taken?"

"Yes, Penelope." There was a touch of annoyance in his voice.

"Whoa," she said. "Remember me, officer Penelope? I'm just doing my job."

"I'm sorry, Penny," he said. "I guess I'm just angry that someone would go into my house while I'm gone. And with...you know. Everything else."

"Be happy that it was when you were gone and not while you were there," she said in all sincerity.

"That's what's upsetting," he said. "I mean, what if they were trying to find me home? Or, you know, someone else?"

That was exactly what Penelope was thinking. Could the break-in at Jacob's house have something to do with what was going on with Doug? She stared at the face on the wanted poster on her desk. "We're dealing with a lot more now," she said.

"Meaning?"

"Camille is dead, Jacob. Murdered."

There was stunned silence on the other end of the line. "I don't want to give you details over the phone..."

"Of course," Jacob said.

"But we are going to have to charge Doug, with the assault on Pete, first of all, but then most likely with Camille's murder too. I don't have a choice, Jacob," she added defensively when she saw the look on his face. "If I don't do it, someone else will."

"Just do you best," Jacob told her. "And trust in God for the rest."

"Always," Penelope said. "Jacob, why don't you stay at my place tonight?" she offered.

"I don't know," he said. "Is that appropriate? What will the neighbors think?"

"The neighbors can think what they want," she snapped. "We are adults and our morality is our own business!"

"I'm just thinking about your reputation..."

Penelope took a breath. "I know you are, Jacob. But everyone already thinks I've been harboring an attempted murderer...how much worse can it get by letting my fiancé sleep in my spare bedroom?"

She heard a touch of humor in his voice. "Well, as long as we're clear that I'm sleeping in the spare bedroom..."

She grinned. "Oh, it's clear all right, mister."

They had a little laugh together. It felt good, to have someone to laugh with, what with everything that was going on. Jacob was her salvation, and in more ways than one. God had done her a good turn with this man.

"When are we going to talk about setting a date?" he

asked.

"I don't know," she teased. "When are we?"

Penny and Jacob had both been avoiding the subject since she had accepted his proposal four months before. It was fun and exciting just being engaged for a while and they had been teasing each other over the prospect of actually pinning down a real date.

"Soon," he said.

"It had better be soon," she replied. "There is no shortage of handsome young doctors out there. So back to tonight. Head over to my place when you're done at the park. You still have your key?"

"I do," he said. "I'll pick up dinner on the way. Will you be home soon?"

"Yeah," said Penelope. "I've just got some forms to fill out."

She didn't mention that the purpose of those forms was to formally charge her best friend of attempted murder.

CHAPTER 20

THAT NIGHT JACOB slept in the guest room bed, and Trevor *camped* on a huge pile of sleeping bags on the floor. She wanted the two of them to sleep in while she had to get up early for her shift.

Exhausted, she slept right through her alarm, finally jerking awake on her own in a panic at six-thirty. She showered and dressed without waking up Jacob and grabbed a quick cup of coffee before leaving for work.

The office looked just like it had last night when she had left it. Maybe she should just put a cot up in the corner, considering the way things were going.

Chief of Police, Curtis Jackson, was already in the building at seven that morning when Penelope showed up. So Penelope was expecting it when Jackson called her into his office. Penelope had wanted to check on Doug first thing, but the Chief took precedence.

Penelope was surprised to see a young man she hadn't met before in a Franklin Police uniform smiling at her from where he stood behind Chief Jackson's desk.

"Officer Penelope Chance," Jackson said to her from his leather armchair, "this here is officer Anthony Ramirez. He's from Tampa and will be joining our team for a while."

Confused, Penelope offered him her hand. "Good to meet you, officer Ramirez. I hope you enjoy your time here with us. Are you, uh, staying long?"

He shook her hand firmly and said, "I'm pleased to meet you, officer. Chief Jackson here graciously agreed to let me do a ride-along for a week. I'd like to relocate to Franklin eventually, but I'm happy to be here now even if it is temporary."

"It will be nice to have another helping hand," Penelope said, "no matter how long you'll be with us."

He smiled broadly. She couldn't help noticing; he was a very good-looking man.

"Did the Chief bring you up to speed, Anthony?" Penelope asked him. "This may not have been the best time for a visit to us."

He nodded, shifting his weight to his other foot. "Seems like a typical week. You've got a couple of cases going on—vandalism, car thefts and so on. Then you've got a guy in the holding cell who tried to run someone down and it looks like he might have killed his ex-wife."

The Chief cleared his throat noisily. Anthony looked down at him, knowing he had done something wrong but not able to figure out what.

"The guy in the cell is my friend," Penelope explained.

"Oh," he said. "Maybe not too typical then."

"Don't worry about it. I've got it covered. There's something else that needs checking on now. Chief, did Jim tell you about the break-in at Jacob's house?"

The Chief nodded. "Got the report this morning. Any ideas?"

Anthony looked at Penelope and said, "If you need some help with this, I've got a clean plate right now. New guy, and all."

Penelope nodded. "Okay. I'll call Jacob in a bit and have him meet you at the house. You have the address off the report?"

Anthony nodded. "Yup. Borrow a cruiser, Chief?"

The Chief quirked an eyebrow at Penelope. "See? He's a go-getter. That's why I want him on our team. Off you go, then. Keys are on the ring in the next room."

Anthony nodded to both of them. He winked at Penelope.

Penelope wasn't sure she had really seen what she saw.

"What do you think?" the Chief asked her.

She waited for the Chief to nod before she said what was on her mind. "Too soon to tell. Seems a little cocky."

The Chief chuckled. "That he does. But he comes highly recommended. Even got a few commendations under his belt. I think he'll make a good addition to our little force here."

"Didn't know there was room in the budget for another officer." Penelope sat down in one of the chairs in front of the Chief's desk. It was going to be another long day. She could feel it already.

Chief Curtis Jackson, man of few words, Chief of Police in their little community for thirty-plus years, smiled a sad smile and shook his head. "There's room in the budget. If someone retires."

"Like who...Wait, you mean you? You're planning on retiring?" The idea of it was hard for Penelope to wrap her head around. For as long as she could remember, when she thought of the Police station, she thought of Curtis. She couldn't picture the place without him.

The Chief shrugged. "Been planning on it. Just didn't know when the time would be right. Seems right to me, now. After this mess with Doug gets cleared up. Where are you at with that?"

"I have some leg work to do today on it, Chief, but the paperwork is filed." The words tasted sour in her mouth.

The Chief leaned forward across his desk. "Look, Penelope. I know you only kept this case because I insisted. But I know, in my heart and in my soul, that you're the right one for it. You think your friend is innocent—go prove it. But if he's not, you do your job, got it?"

Penelope nodded, unable to answer.

"Good. Because when I'm gone, I'm going to need

someone to take my place. And I want that someone to be you, Penelope."

Penelope sat without speaking, digesting what the Chief had just said, for a few heartbeats. "You want me to what?"

"You heard me. There's no one else suitable. Just you. Unless Doug's mess becomes your own. Do your job. Do it right. Hear me?"

Penelope nodded. "Chief, I always do."

CHAPTER 21

PENELOPE MADE A quick call to Jacob to let him know that a new officer was coming over to start the investigation on the break-in to his house. They talked for a little while, but Penelope did not say anything about the Chief retiring or wanting Penelope to take over for him. It all still seemed too big. Plus, Curtis wanting her to be Chief wouldn't make it so. The Town Council and the Mayor would have to sign off on it. So it was best not to count those particular chickens before they hatched. Jacob had arranged for his aunt Jessie to watch Trevor and he was going into the clinic after making his police report.

While officer Anthony Ramirez was checking out her fiancé's house, Penelope went out to begin talking to the townspeople so that she could nail down a timeline of who saw what and when they saw it.

She already knew the approximate times when Doug was at The Pizza Palace and Ricky's Pub, so she was looking for someone else to verify them. Someone who knew something more. That elusive bit of information that she knew was there but just couldn't see. If she was lucky, there would be a few folks from each location who could help her.

Before she had left, she'd filled the Chief in on the angle she had on Camille's boyfriend. The Chief said he'd call the police over in Gainesville and let them know about it, and then coordinate a search for this guy. If he even existed, that is. The Chief thought it might just be Doug blowing smoke. Penelope wasn't so sure. Doug had lied to her once already—and while she had been sure of their friendship before all this started, now she had to question it. Was Doug telling the truth about Findley? Well, this was how she was going to find out.

Penelope started at The Pizza Palace. By now it was nearing eleven o'clock and they opened their doors at ten, so the crowd was still light on a mid-morning Monday and the staff had the time to talk to her. She asked the waitress if anyone else was there at the same time as Doug last Friday evening. The waitress thought for a moment and then told her the names of three regulars. Penelope wrote the names down. She knew each one, and knew they'd recognize Doug if they'd seen him.

Then the waitress, Mandy Blonkin, a good woman who Penelope knew was holding down two jobs to support her family, told her something that made her pen slip. "There was a really creepy guy in here, too, that day," she said. "He sat in the back booth and kept staring at Doug, but I don't think Doug saw him."

"Why do you say that?" Penelope asked.

"Doug was in one of the front booths on the other side and was facing away from Mr. Creepy," she answered, shrugging. "The guy sure looked like he was mad about something."

"Can you describe him for me?" Penelope asked.

Mandy thought for a moment and said, "You're asking a lot at this point, Penelope. Um. I guess he was about six-foot, I don't know, maybe shorter. But he had black hair and his nose was bent like it had been broken a couple of times. He had an awful snake tattoo on his right hand. The thing looked downright evil." She shuddered. "He kind of grinned when he saw I didn't like it."

Michael Findley. She was describing the man from the wanted poster Doug had given her. The wanted poster of Camille's current boyfriend, supposedly. There's no way that could be a coincidence.

But if the man was in town, that was trouble. Especially if he'd been stalking Doug the night of the attack on Pete.

She thanked Mandy for the information with what she hoped was a poker face, and then set out to speak with the three other people who had pizza for dinner on Friday night.

Hard to believe that all of this had happened over one weekend.

The first was a retired widower, Mr. Blane Morris. Penelope had grown up knowing Blane. The man used to let her and Doug pick loquats off of his tree when they were both kids. Blane told Penelope that he remembered seeing Doug come into the restaurant at about five that evening, maybe a few minutes later. He had been getting ready to leave when Doug walked in.

Penelope asked if he remembered anyone looking out of place.

"Oh, yes," Blane said. "There was a stranger, an angry young man with some tattoos—looked like he'd been in a fight or two over the years. Rough looking, you know. Kinda gave me a shove as he came in."

Penelope nodded and kept her smile in place even as her insides twisted. Angry young man. Could it be the same guy that Mandy the waitress had seen?

Blane sucked on his dentures as he continued. "So I kept an eye on him for a minute in case he was planning to rob them, but he went to the last booth in the back and just sat down. Didn't bother anyone. Just sat there and scowled."

Penelope shook the man's hand. "Thank you, sir. You've been very helpful. How's the leg doing you these days?"

Blane, in his younger days, had served in the military. He'd loved to tell Penelope stories about those days, and

Penelope would sit on the man's porch for hours and listen to him. His leg had been hit with several pieces of shrapnel during World War II and had given him a permanent limp.

"It pains me during heavy rains. Can always tell when a storm's coming." He shook Penelope's hand. "Think one's coming now, officer Chance."

Penelope couldn't help hearing a double meaning in the old man's words as she shook his hand. Things were building up, and a storm was coming.

The next two people on her list were a young married couple. Gail and Hank Carpenter remembered Friday evening the same way. They remembered Doug coming into The Pizza Palace. They even remembered Blane Morris leaving and being nearly knocked down by a rude and angry man. According to them, the man went and sat in the back, near them, glaring at Doug. The Carpenters left a little before six, and Doug stood in line behind them to pay.

"We heard about what happened the next day," Hank said, "and we remembered how we had just seen Doug in there. I hope you can put him away for what happened. He's bringing a bad element to this town."

Penelope nodded, keeping her face neutral. Not everyone in town knew about Doug being Penelope's friend, apparently. But either way, the events of this weekend had kept the memory of seeing Doug at The Pizza Palace fresh in their minds, so that helped. They didn't have a detailed description of the angry man, but it backed up Blane and Mandy's story, and both of them did have a good description.

Of Michael Findley.

The other side of this coin was a little brighter. She had good confirmation from four different witnesses that Doug was at The Pizza Palace from five until almost six o'clock. That fit with what Doug had given her as a timeline for that night. Penelope knew exactly where Doug was for the entire end of his night. He was at The Last Chance Tavern, where Penelope had found him after getting the report that their poor friend Pete Lamb had been run down, supposedly by Doug.

Doug had told her that he'd only had the one beer, with food, by the time he'd left The Pizza Palace, and Mandy the waitress verified that. Given his height and weight and tolerance for alcohol, there was no way he could have been drunk when he left.

She had already interviewed Rick Ferrero, owner of Ricky's Pub, the next place that Doug said he went to after The Pizza Palace, so Penelope decided to knock on the doors of nearby houses.

This was the part of police work that didn't get shown a lot on the television shows. Hard legwork, asking questions of people and coming up dry time and again before you found what you were looking for. At the third house one block behind Ricky's Pub, Mrs. Betsy Isaacs suggested that the man across the street, Dan Hughes, may know something because, as she stated it, "He walks that vicious little Pomeranian of his at a quarter 'til six every evening. Mouthy little mutt."

Thanking her for her help and cooperation, Penelope turned to leave. "He's not at home right now," she said. "He went to Jacksonville on Sunday to visit his mother. Still gone."

"Did you see him leave yesterday?"

"No, I didn't," Mrs. Isaacs replied with a small shrug, "but his car's not there. Sometimes he stays until the next day. He should be back by suppertime, though. He's gotta walk that dog, you know."

Penelope thanked her again and went back to her car. She had a feeling the neighbor with his noisy dog might have the information she was looking for, so she planned to come back later in the evening. The feeling that she was on the right track lingered. She took it as a good sign.

CHAPTER 22

RETURNING TO THE police station, Penelope went directly to Chief Jackson's office. She knocked and soon heard the Chief tell her to come in. Closing the door behind her, she sat down in the same chair she'd been in that morning. "We've got a problem," she started to say.

Chief Jackson waved her to silence. "Go ahead, Detective Greene," he said, and it was then that Penelope realized the Police was on a conference call.

"Who's that there with you?" the voice over the line said. Penelope recognized the booming bass tone immediately.

"Donny Greene," Penelope said, a little louder so that the phone would pick up her voice. "Haven't seen you in a dog's age."

"Penelope Chance!" Donny said cheerfully. "I haven't

seen or heard from you since you got engaged to that handsome Doctor Jacob Gordon. When's the first little Penelope due?"

Penelope laughed at her old friend. "We haven't even set the date yet, Donny. I'll be doing that in a few more months. Jacob said he's willing to have ten kids, but I think two or three would be more than enough. I'll be sure to send you an invitation to the wedding, though. So what's up?"

The Chief was the one who answered him. "Michael Findley."

The hair on the back of Penelope's neck stood up.

"He's our prime suspect in the Foster murder case. We can't find him over here," Donny explained. "Anywhere. But, we confirmed that the victim was living with him. A lot of his things are still in their house. The Chief was telling us that you are taking care of her son."

"Yeah, that's right. Camille dropped him off to her ex-husband before going back to Gainesville and ending up dead. Her ex is in a lot of trouble now as it is, Donny. But put all that aside for a minute. I know why you can't find this Findley character."

"Why's that?"

The Police looked at her, waiting.

"Because he's here...or at least he was on Friday night," Penelope explained. "That's what I was coming in to tell you, Chief. I've got at least two people who can identify him positively, and two others who probably could if I showed them a picture."

There was silence in the room and on the phone line.

Then the Chief asked, "Do we know where he is now?"

Penelope shook her head. "No, we don't. I'm looking into a few things and I'll know more soon. Donny, do you have the time of death yet?"

"Not yet. A really bad multi-car pile up on the interstate has the Medical Examiner backed up," the Detective answered.

"Sorry to hear that Donny," Penelope replied. "Chief, I've buttoned down the timeline for Doug on Friday, at least for the early part of the evening."

"And after that?" the Chief asked her.

"I don't know yet," Penelope had to admit.

The Chief nodded. "Detective Greene, we'll get back to you when we know more. Do the same for us, all right?"

"Will do, Chief. Penelope, you still there?"

"I'm here Donny."

"You have to know that the ex also looks good to us for this murder, right?" Penelope could hear the apologetic tone in Donny's voice.

"Yeah, I know that. We're holding him here on our own attempted murder charges. He's not going anywhere."

"Okay." There was a long pause. "Good luck with this, Penelope."

"No such thing as luck, Donny."

"Only faith." The two laughed at their old joke. For Penelope, it wasn't just a joke. It was the truth.

* * *

When Penelope finished going over what she had found out so far with the Chief, she left his office with the intention of going to check on Doug. She knew how lonely the holding area was when it was just you back there, being watched on a monitor by the person at the front desk.

Officer Anthony Ramirez had returned to the police station to write his preliminary report and she found him now sitting at her desk, using her computer. He smiled at her when he saw her coming out, holding up the freshly printed report to her. "Officer, I didn't find anything other than an unlocked window to the spare bedroom. No sign of forced entry, so I'm guessing the window was our perp's way in."

"Did you check for footprints or fingerprints?" she asked him, accepting the report and reading it over.

"Of course," he replied, leaning back in a way that accentuated his muscular physique, "and there's a good one on the side of his house. Looks like he braced himself to climb in. Came back for a fingerprint kit. Know where they are?"

"In the back of the cruisers," she told him. "We keep one in each. Why do you think the person who did this is a guy?"

"Big boot print. Most likely a guy. If all he took was photos then I'm guessing he knew someone in them."

That idea had occurred to Penelope. Jacob had said the photos were of him, her, Doug and Camille. Someone knew one of those people, obviously. Most likely, with everything else going on, Doug or Camille.

"Good job, officer," Penelope said, coming back to herself. "Uh, see if Saunders or Petersen can help you out with that angle."

"Aw," he said, actually sounding disappointed. "I was hoping you and me maybe could get a chance to work together."

Penelope took his meaning, clear as day. She needed to nip that in the bud. "Did you meet with Jacob out at his house?"

Anthony nodded. "Nice guy. Good head on his shoulders. He a friend of yours?"

"He's my fiancé."

The light came on in Anthony's eyes and he smiled suggestively. "Are you saying I'm too late?"

"That is exactly what I am saying."

Anthony nodded at her. "I'll take that under consideration then. So, your fiancé," he twisted the word a little, but Penelope didn't rise to the bait, "was telling me a little about your relationship with Doug Foster. I hope you figure this thing out. I don't know what I would do if my brother ever got into that kind of trouble."

Penelope was happy to be back on safe conversation ground. "Well, Doug's not my natural brother." Anthony gave her a questioning look and she added, "My parents died when I was eight. Neither of them had any relatives who were able to take on a child. My parents and Doug's parents were good friends, so his parents adopted and raised me. I was an only child until then and he's the closest thing I've had to any real family."

"What happened to your parents?" he asked, innocently enough.

Penelope blinked away an image of their house, in flames, falling down on itself as the fire department tried to save it. "I'll tell you that some other time," she said to him. "For now, let's just leave it at me and Doug being as close to blood as two people can get without being actually related."

"That's all the reason you need to want to solve this," Anthony said.

She nodded. Penelope wondered why she had opened up to him about this. Jacob knew all about it, of course, and so did most long-time residents of Franklin.

"Is there anything I can do to help with this case?" he asked, his neutral face hard to read.

"I've got it. For now. You keep on this burglary. Scare up some leads."

"You've got it, officer Chance," he said, again flashing that smile. She watched him leave the room and looked away when he turned to see if she was watching him.

Her face grew warm and she chided herself for being distracted.

Please God, Penelope asked, *help me to stay the course. I took up this career hoping to do Your work, hoping to help other people. Now the one who needs my help is my friend, Doug. Help me to ignore temptation and distraction alike. Help me to keep my mind focused. Help me do my best. And if it is Your will, Lord God, help me show my friend is innocent.*

She knew that last part was a little selfish. But it was what was in her heart. God never asked for more than that.

Jacob would be at the clinic by now, so Penelope decided to check on whether he knew if Pete was due to come back from Grace Memorial Hospital in Gainesville. She was hopeful Pete would make a quick recovery and help button up some of the loose ends that seemed to be sprouting everywhere she looked.

Pete was one of those people that everyone was aware of, but no one really knew. He was only a couple of years older than Penelope and Doug, but their paths didn't cross often when they were growing up. Penelope and Doug were typical kids doing typical kid stuff, but Pete was the loner type and kept to himself most of the time. The fact that Pete's father was an alcoholic, domineering tyrant certainly had some influence on him.

Penelope and Doug were aware that Pete began sneaking alcohol out of the house and drinking around age twelve. It was simply something they accepted and they never asked why. Pete never volunteered the information either.

CHAPTER 23

"NO, PENNY, I'M not sure when Pete will be released," Jacob told her over the phone. "I got a call from Grace Memorial a little while ago. Still no sign of internal injuries and no sign of brain swelling, but they want him to rest due to those cracked ribs. He's fighting them because he wants a drink, so there is the matter of detox as well."

"Is Patty still with him?" he asked Jacob.

"Yes she is. Ever the loyal sister."

"How did Trevor take to Aunt Jessie."

Jacob chuckled. "He loved her. She bribed him with brownies, so I can't say it was impartial."

"You know, I got to talk to Donny Greene today. You remember him? He asked when you and I were going to have children."

"Uh, he's kind of jumping the gun, isn't he?" he said with a laugh.

"Yeah, well. Always good to plan ahead. Don't you agree, Doc?"

"I surely do, officer beautiful. I'm thinking we're going to have to put an addition onto your house. Two bedrooms aren't going to be enough for five or six kids…"

Penelope laughed. "Slow down there," she said. "We'll try one and see how it goes."

"Or we could move into my house," he offered. "Four bedrooms, no waiting."

She sighed. "No security system and one faulty window."

"So, about that," he said, "Did officer Ramirez find anything yet?"

"He's out there with a fingerprint kit now. It's a long shot, but he likes to go that extra mile, I think. So hopefully we'll know something before too much longer." She paused, and then casually asked, "What did you think of him?"

"What did I think of him?" She could almost feel Jacob calculating the weight of her question in his head. "Well, he seems like a competent enough police officer. And we talked for a bit. Why?"

"No reason," she said.

"There's always a reason. I did get a little vibe from him," Jacob said. "Almost like he was sizing me up and deciding he was…I don't know. Better than me? Better looking? Something like that."

"Yeah," she said.

"It's a thing guys do, you know," he assured her. "We've all got some of that competitiveness in us. A little macho posturing...You want me to beat him up, challenge him to a duel or something?"

Penelope giggled. "No! Of course not!"

"You sure? I am ready to stand up for my woman."

"I'm sure you are, Tarzan," Penelope said. "I'm sure that won't be necessary."

"Alright. You let me know if he looks at you funny and you change your mind."

"Ok, I will. I love you, Jacob," she said to him.

"I love you back."

She hung up the phone.

Only to have it ring again.

"Franklin Police station, officer Chance speaking," she said by rote.

It was officer Ramirez. "Ma'am," he said, "you may want to come out to Jacob's house. There's something here I think you should see."

"What is it, Anthony?" she asked. More distractions, she thought to herself. Just what she didn't need. "You really need me there for this?"

God help me, she prayed silently.

"I'd rather you see it for yourself," he insisted.

"Fine," she sighed, giving up on her idea of talking with Doug. "I'll be there in a few."

* * *

Officer Ramirez met Penelope at the driveway and motioned her around to the back of Jacob's house without a word. He pointed out the imprint of a shoe on the siding just below the window and all the fingerprints he was able to find and lift.

"You see those imprints in the dirt there?" he asked.

"Looks like he used a ladder," she said.

"Where would he get a ladder?" Anthony asked.

She looked at him, and then over his shoulder at the detached garage that served as Jacob's garden shed and workroom. Anthony smiled and walked back there.

Penelope followed. The door was unlocked. Anthony swung it open using his flashlight.

What she saw surprised her. Someone had stayed for a while. There was a sleeping bag, cigarette butts scattered about, a six pack's worth of empty beer cans and fast food wrappers on the floor. Right there next to the sleeping bag was the framed photo from Jacob's wall.

Penelope ground her teeth as she surveyed the room. She thought she probably knew exactly who had been staying there. She looked at officer Ramirez. "We can't tell Jacob about this just yet," she said.

"Why not? It's Jacob's house and he should know what's going on."

Penelope shook her head. "This is the way we do this, officer Ramirez. We don't tell Jacob anything about this yet. We're going to set up and watch the place, and when he comes back, we'll get him. Then we tell Jacob."

Anthony cocked his head and looked at her. "You seem to be pretty sure you know who 'he' is?"

"I am," she said.

"You want to share this with your fellow officer? Just so that I know what I'm getting into here?"

"Michael Findley."

Anthony grinned. "The main suspect in the Foster murder in Gainesville."

Penelope nodded.

Anthony's grin remained. "And they told me I was gonna be bored in this quiet little town..."

"Hopefully, after this week, you will be."

Penelope helped him clean up the fingerprint powder from the window. She didn't want Findley to know the police had been here. They returned to the station to fill in Chief Jackson and set up a stakeout. She was excited to be on track to solving the mysteries that Doug seemed to keep getting entrapped in.

Not even a half hour later, they were back on Jacob's street in an unmarked car and parked a few houses down in such a way that they had a good view of his back yard and the shed. If everything worked out well, Findley wouldn't know they had been there. She'd sent Jim Saunders to check on Jacob's house last night, but she knew from reading Anthony's report that Jim had only done a drive-by and then a perimeter sweep of the house later in the night. There was no reason for an intruder to be spooked by that.

Anthony sat in the passenger seat of Penelope's Jetta. They drank from styrofoam cups of coffee and watched out the windshield as the day wore on. They'd picked up sandwiches from Little LuLu's on their way through, and lunch was eaten in relative silence. And still there was no sign of the intruder.

Penelope was used to doing this kind of work. It was almost what police work was actually like, in the real world. A lot of sitting and waiting and praying things worked out. However, it was obvious that officer Ramirez was more used to action than waiting, and a police force with enough money for sophisticated equipment.

"Gah!" he exclaimed, putting the remains of his sandwich back in its paper bag sleeve. "Can't we set up a camera to do this?"

Penelope nodded, slowly. "We could. We'd have to requisition one from Gainesville, have the techs set it up, draw a huge amount of attention to ourselves, tip off Findley and he'd slip away right under our noses. I know this is old-school. This is how it works out here."

She could feel him looking at her intently. "And this is how you like it?"

"It is," she answered without looking at him. "So what made you become a police officer?"

Penelope saw his flashy grin return. "Are you curious about me, officer Chance?"

"People become police officers for different reasons. Some people want the power that authority gives. Some people have a martyr complex and want to burn themselves out in a burst of glory. Other people have an honest desire to do good things for other people. There are a lot of reasons, and not all of them are good. If you're going to come and work for us here in Franklin, I'd like to know what we're getting." She turned and looked him squarely in the eyes. "So what's your reason?"

"Well, officer Chance, I suppose the smart answer is to say that I have an honest desire to do good things for other people. Right?"

"Okay, that would be the good answer in a job interview." She used a pair of hunting binoculars and scanned the area around Jacob's house. "Now, what's the real reason?"

"You really want to know?"

"I wouldn't be asking if I didn't want to know."

"Fine. Here's the story. I grew up on the wrong side of Miami. Everyone was a criminal. Gangs, petty thieves, drug users, drug dealers. My dad died in a drive-by shooting when I was fifteen. Wrong place at the wrong time. My momma did her best to keep it together after that, you know. Sent us to church, kept us fed and clean. Then she got cancer and died too. My younger brothers and my sister went into foster care. But I was eighteen. I promised myself I'd get out of there. This seemed like the best way to do it."

Penelope nodded. "That wasn't an easy way to grow up," she acknowledged. "I'm glad you chose a better path."

Anthony seemed uncomfortable. "So am I up to your standards?" he asked with a hint of sarcasm.

Was that a shadow behind the house? Penelope focused the binoculars again. "The question is are you up to your own standards? It's not up to me. It's your path. The only one who can tell if your journey fits you, besides God, is you. Your situation is unique. You'll make of it what you will. Good? Bad? That's up to you. You don't seem to be in it for the glory or the authority, and those are the worst reasons to do it."

Yes, definitely a shadow. "So I guess you'll show us what kind of police officer you are in your own time. We've got movement now. Get ready."

Anthony stared at her, his mouth open. She'd surprised him, obviously. Penelope thought she saw something shift in his focus, in the way he looked at her, but it might have just been the excitement of the moment.

Michael Findley was walking through Jacob's yard.

CHAPTER 24

POLICE TRAINING WAS a funny thing.

Most of what a police officer trains for are things that might happen. Circumstances that might arise. Police had to be trained to use their firearm, for instance, but very rarely in an officer's career do they ever have the need to use it. Police have to be trained in emergency operation, just in case they get in a car chase. Things like that. It was a big game of what if.

As Penelope and Anthony approached Jacob's shed from opposite sides, her training kicked in. Stay low. Draw your weapon but keep your finger off the trigger until ready to fire. Use your cover. In this way, they ended up at opposite corners of the front of the shed. Silently, she motioned for him to take a position to the right of the door.

She prayed quickly to God for her safety and Anthony's safety, and that no one here would be hurt. *God help me do what I have to do*, she added.

One look at Anthony showed him alert and ready to proceed. She nodded at him once, and then banged loudly on the door of the shed with her weapon ready. "Michael Findley," she said. "This is the police. Come out with your hands up!"

Michael Findley did not come out with his hands up. There were sounds of scrambling, and objects scattering.

A loud crash came from inside and Anthony whirled around.

Findley was coming out the side window of the shed.

Anthony yelled. "Drop the weapon! Drop the weapon!"

Penelope rounded the corner to see Findley on the ground with Anthony kneeling on his back.

"Okay!" Findley stopped struggling. "You got me. You got me! I give up!"

Somehow Penelope didn't believe him. "Anthony? You need help getting him cuffed?"

"I got it," he shouted.

Penelope stood by with her weapon ready.

And then Anthony cried out and swore loudly but remained on top of Findley. Training kicked in. Holstering her weapon, Penelope threw herself on top of Findley and with a twist and a roll she ended up sitting on the man's leg with an ankle-lock in place. She twisted a centimeter more and heard Findley cry out in pain.

"Drop the knife! Now!" Penelope hollered at the top of her voice.

Findley dropped the knife and the two of them got him cuffed.

"Anthony? You okay?" It was then that Penelope saw the slice through his blue uniform shirt and the red that stained the edges of the cut.

"You're hurt," she said.

"It's not bad. He surprised me, is all." He stood up. "Coulda been worse. Glad you were here, officer." His grin returned. "We make a good team."

"Well done, officer," Penelope said. Saying a silent thank-you to the Lord for protecting them, she stood up as well.

"You've got a lot to answer for, Findley."

"I didn't kill my girlfriend," the man said immediately, turning an angry glare on Penelope.

"Thanks for clearing that up," she said. "I guess we can release you now."

Findley's smile was cold and angry. "I know what's going on. Don't think I don't. You and Doug are friends, and you want to put this on me. But I'm telling you right now, wasn't me."

"Then who, seeing as how you're being so helpful all of a sudden?" Anthony asked, dragging Findley to his feet.

"Why, Doug Foster of course. He killed my girlfriend.

His ex-wife. Mother of his child. He did it. I come here to make sure he goes down for it."

CHAPTER 25

OFFICER SAUNDERS RESPONDED to Jacob's house to pick up Findley in a cruiser. Back at the station, Chief Jackson was there to meet them.

"So that's him?" the Chief asked Penelope.

"Yes, sir. Michael Findley. In the flesh."

"Where is officer Ramirez?"

"I dropped him off at the clinic."

"What happened?"

"Findley cut him with a knife while we were arresting him." Jim Saunders brought Findley out of the back of his car and took him up the stairs into the station. What would be next on Penelope's list of things to do was interviewing that guy.

The Chief nodded, frowning. "So Findley was in town. That sort of supports Doug's story. At least it agrees with the witness statements. That must make you happy, Penelope."

"I'd be happy about it if he'd confess. I don't know, sir. There's something going on here that I'm missing. I just can't figure out what."

The Chief laid a hand on her shoulder. "I've got faith in you, Penelope."

"And I've got faith in God, so it should work out, right?" Penelope walked next to the Chief as they went inside behind Jim.

"Everything always works out. Just not the way we expect," the Chief said.

Penelope knew the truth of that, but she was still hopeful for a particular outcome, one where Doug was found to be innocent, and the real bad guy would go to jail for a very, very long time.

She didn't like to think about what would happen if things went the other way.

But, her next step to finding the truth would be to interrogate Findley. The Chief went to his office to call over to Gainesville and let them know Findley was in their custody here. Penelope went to the other part of the building where the interrogation room was, the same place where she had been talking with Doug, the previous day.

Jim was there, watching over Findley through the two-way mirror. The Officer yawned, his handlebar mustache stretching out with his face.

"You should go home and get some sleep," Penelope said to him. "I know there's a lot going on and it's all hands on deck, but you do know that you can't live here, don't you?"

"You're one to talk," Jim said with a grin and rubbed at his eyes. "Chief told me I could work as many hours as I can handle. Gonna need the money soon. Anna and I just found out we're going to have another baby."

Penelope did a double take. Jim and his wife already had one child, and after a very hard labor, the doctors over in Gainesville had told her that she might never conceive again. She hadn't even known they had been trying. "Congratulations, Jim!" she said. "That's great news."

"I'd like a boy this time," Saunders said, "but honestly, so long as the baby's healthy, I'll be a happy dad."

Penelope shook Jim's hand, honestly happy for him. Another happy couple with their children. Earlier, when Donny Greene had asked when she and Jacob would have kids, she had kind of laughed the question off. She remembered growing up without a family, and when she was being honest with herself she knew she was scared she might visit that trouble on her own children some day. But watching Doug with Trevor, and now seeing Jim as an expectant father again, Penelope knew in her heart that the decision she had made with Jacob to start a family once they were married was the right choice to make.

"Are you going to stay and watch this?" she asked Jim, motioning to the interview room and its one occupant, handcuffed to the chair on both sides.

"Yup. Can't wait to see how this turns out."

"Okay. Here we go, then."

Penelope entered the room with her notepad and pen after flicking the switch on the outside of the room first, turning on the surveillance camera.

She sat down across from Findley at the metal table. The man's hands were both handcuffed to an arm of the chair, and the chair was bolted to the floor. She was in no danger from him. She wrote a heading for her notes, noted the time and jotted it down, and with a deep breath she started.

"You and I are going to have a talk now, Findley. But I have to read you your Miranda warnings first. You understand that?"

"I didn't kill Camille, officer. You've got no reason to hold me. None." Findley smiled at her in that same aggravating way he had back at Jacob's house.

"I've got no reason to hold you? Seriously?" Penelope leaned back in her chair, letting herself get a little off track. "How about committing a burglary and trespassing, in violation of eight-one-oh-point-oh-two and eight-one-oh-point-oh-eight of the Florida criminal statute? What about aggravated charge upon a police officer, in violation of section seven-eighty-four-point-oh-seven? Oh, and then there's that small matter of the state of California wanting you for armed robbery. And for questioning in a murder case," she added pointedly. "I think I've got plenty of reason to hold you. What I don't have is some explanation for how your girlfriend ended up dead."

Findley sat back now too, glaring at Penelope, his eyes narrowed over that broken and crooked nose.

"So, like I said. I need to read you your Miranda warnings. You have the right to remain silent. If you give up the right to remain silent, anything you say can and will be used against you in court. You have the right to talk to a lawyer before answering any of my questions. If you cannot afford to hire a lawyer, one will be appointed for you without cost and before any questioning. And, you have the right to use any of these rights at any time you want during this interview." She looked up from her card when she was done. "Do you understand each of these rights as I have read them to you?"

"Sure," Findley shrugged. "I've heard 'em on TV."

"Good. See? We're getting along great already."

"I didn't kill her."

"Yeah. You said that already. Does that mean you want to talk to me, Mr. Findley?" Penelope was trying to get under the guy's skin, trying to make him mad, hoping that something would trip up.

"I'm talking to you now, ain't I?" Findley said.

"Where were you when it happened?" Penelope asked, writing down his time of Miranda and Findley's consent to talk.

"I was already over here in Franklin."

Penelope wrote out more notes, nodding, listening.

Findley continued on. "That was Friday night. I was following Doug around town."

"And why was that?" Penelope asked.

"Because Camille said she was going to leave me and go back to him. I wanted to see what kind of a guy he was. If he was good enough for her."

"Well, you know, that fits in with what we know already. We have witnesses from The Pizza Palace who saw you in there at the same time as Doug. And they did say you were watching him."

Findley smiled again, a smile that said he thought he was winning. "See? There you go. I was right here the whole day."

"Can anyone confirm you were here before supper time?" Penelope asked.

"What?"

Penelope stopped writing and looked up at the man across from him. "You said you were here the whole day. Can anyone," she said again, slowly, "confirm you were in town before five o'clock? The people at The Pizza Palace saw you there at the same time as Doug. Okay, fine. What about before that?"

Findley shrugged. "I don't know who might have seen me. Ask around. That's your job."

"Good idea. I'll do that." Penelope wrote some more. "And after The Pizza Palace? Where did you go?"

"I kept following Doug. That man was about to ruin my relationship with a great woman who I loved dearly and I wanted to see what he was up to."

Penelope wrote that down exactly as Findley had said it, but she also made a note that the words sounded practiced, as though they were being recited from memory. "So you followed Doug from The Pizza Palace. Then what?"

"He went to this little bar called Ricky's Pub."

So far, Findley was corroborating Doug's story.

"He went in, had a beer," Findley continued. "Finished his beer and then went outside."

Penelope's heart sank. "So where did he go?"

Findley shook his hands in the cuffs, making them rattle against the metal arms of the chair. Penelope noticed that the man's knuckles were all scraped up.

"Can we get these off, maybe?" he asked.

"No," Penelope said flatly. "What did you see Doug do then, Mr. Findley?"

"I don't know."

"You didn't follow him? I thought that was the purpose of your trip."

"Man's gotta eat and Ricky's place serves a mean bowl of conch chowder. I figured he just forgot his wallet or phone or something in his fancy truck and went out to get it. But he didn't come back for over an hour."

Over an hour? Penelope thought to herself. *If Camille was murdered Friday night, that was more than enough time too for Doug to get to Gainesville and back. But what about Trevor? How did he get here? Did Doug bring him back to his house and leave him there Friday night? Maybe that's why Trevor was lost...*

Too many questions. Things still weren't adding up.

Penelope focused her thoughts and continued. "So what happened then?"

Findley grinned and said, "Doug came back with his truck all beat up as if he'd run into something."

Penelope stopped cold. This wasn't helping Doug.

"Then," Findley continued, "he had another beer and left again. This time I followed him to some dive called The Last Chance Tavern."

"And what did you do then?"

"I drove off and left him there. I seen all I needed to see. I knew what kind of man he was then. The guy's a drunk. Scum. Lowlife. He didn't deserve Camille and there was no way she'd ever leave me for a guy like that."

"You mean, with you being such an upstanding citizen and all?" Penelope said sarcastically.

"Hey, I did some crimes, sure. But I always treated Camille right. She had nothing to fear from me."

"Not like those other people in those other assault charges, you mean? And not before she decided to leave you for Doug." Penelope figured that gave Findley a good motive. But if Findley was here, in town, when the murder happened, then that kind of left one person on the hook—Doug.

Findley didn't say anything else—just sat there, smiling.

"So, where did you go then?" Penelope asked, still writing notes.

" I wanted to give Camille some time to cool off before I went home, so I went and broke into the doctor's shed. Needed a place to stay. Decided to stay the weekend. No one's ever there. Not sure where that man sleeps at night..." He winked at Penelope.

Penelope fisted her hand around her pen and counted to ten in her mind to relax. This guy had no idea what Jacob was to her, did he?

"I knew who he was, of course," Findley was saying. "He was a friend of Camille's. Camille talked about him all the time. He was at her and Doug's wedding. He's a doctor, so I knew what kind of hours he worked and how the house would be empty most of the time. When I got in there I scoped the place out and saw the photos on the wall, with Camille in them, so I took one. If Camille's gonna leave me, I wanted something to remember her by."

"You sure you didn't take them to remember her after she was dead?" Penelope asked him.

Findley just shook his head. The arrogance the man displayed was monumental. "Nope. Far as I knew, she was still alive and just leaving me. I wanted to give her some space to do that."

Penelope sat back and regarded Findley. All the

words seemed to fit, except for one glaring discrepancy. But Penelope was more interested in the way the man spoke. It was the way he used words like weapons to defend himself against every accusation. The way he had every answer ready and prepped. Penelope knew Findley was lying.

But did she have enough evidence to prove it?

"You're lying," she told the man flat out.

Findley grinned and shook his head. "I'm lying about what? What? You tell me anything you can prove is a lie. Go on, you tell me right now!"

"See, Mr. Findley, you think you have everything prepared, and that's actually what's tripping you up." Penelope leaned forward some, her hands resting casually on the table. "You're playing kind of a shell game, moving information from here to there and expecting no one to notice." Penelope turned over one hand at a time to demonstrate. "Right hand, left hand. They have to both know what the other is doing, or it all falls apart."

Findley leaned back calmly. "You tell me one lie I've made. Go on. Tell me."

"The biggest lie of all, Mr. Findley. You lied about not killing Camille."

That smile returned and Penelope so wanted to slap it off the man's face! But she buried her anger, and did her job.

"So how do you know I'm lying about that, officer?" Findley asked her with a sneer.

"Because," Penelope answered, "when I asked you where you were when she was killed, you gave me an exact answer. You never asked me when it happened. You already knew."

CHAPTER 26

SHE QUESTIONED FINDLEY about the other things he had done, getting admissions about the attack on officer Ramirez and that Findley knew there was a warrant out for his arrest from California, and then decided to take a break.

"Nice job," Jim Saunders told her. He'd watched from the other side of the two-way mirror.

Penelope didn't feel she'd done a nice job. "I've only established a time line for Friday night. I still need to question him about his whereabouts on Saturday and Sunday," Penelope said sharply. "As far as Camille's murder is concerned, we still need time of death from the Medical Examiner. Right now we're working with a thirty-six hour window, so the murder could've taken place on Saturday or even late Friday night. I'll give him a couple hours to stew and then see if he sticks to his story."

She would have to go back out to speak to Dan Hughes. Hopefully the man with his little dog would be home by now, and he would have seen something on Friday night. Hopefully. But first Penelope needed to go and talk to Doug. And to call Jacob, of course. Anthony would have filled him in by now, but she wanted to let him know the finer details and reassure him that everything was all right.

Back in the holding cell area Penelope found Doug lying down on the metal bench behind his bars. He looked as though he was asleep. His eyes were closed, and he was breathing evenly. With all the stress he was under, Penelope knew he must be exhausted. She didn't bother trying to wake him.

She asked Jim to keep an eye on Findley while she went out for a while. Officer Peterson was due at work for the night shift in a few hours. Jim promised to watch the guy and to have Peterson do the same if he got there before Penelope got back.

On her way out to Dan Hughes' house, she called Jacob. He didn't pick up until the fifth ring. "Hey handsome," she said when he answered. "Busy day over there?"

"Well, I have a police officer with a nice slice across his shoulder that required fifteen stitches to close. Plus a young kid who spilled out on his bicycle—a champion road-rash. Mr. Gainey got a compound fracture in his leg falling off a ladder—had to send him to Grace Memorial to get it set. Oh. And I've got a guy in here who swears he fell down some stairs. But I'm pretty sure he's been beat up. Maybe you want to swing by and see him?"

"Wish I could, honey. I've got to go and see a potential witness in Doug's case. Did Anthony tell you what happened with your house break-in?" She slowed for a stop sign at an intersection and waved an old man to cross the street.

"Yes, he did. You have no idea how creeped out I am to think that guy was actually living in my back yard."

"I don't know. Try not to think about it. We've got him in custody now and he's not going anywhere for a long time. You want to stay at my house for a while?"

He hesitated, but she already knew what his answer would be. "I've made an appointment to get a security system installed, but it'll be a few days. I'll stay until then, thanks. I can help out with Trevor. I've got to practice taking care of a kid, don't I?"

She smiled. "Yes, you do." The elderly gentleman made it to the other sidewalk, and turned and waved to Penelope.

"If I can take care of one I can take care of ten..."

"Let's start with one, okay? You might feel differently about it then." She eased forward into the intersection.

"Doubtful. The world can't have too many little Penelopes running around."

"You mean it can't have too many little Jacobs?"

He laughed again, and she was happy to hear he was feeling better after the violation of his home by Michael Findley. "So tell me," she said, adjusting the volume on her hands-free set. "What's the name of the guy you think got beat up?"

"Dan Hughes," he answered.

Penelope braked so hard that the tires squealed. "Jacob, do not let that man leave your clinic until I get there," she told him, spinning the car into a u-turn in the middle of Main Street. Heads turned to watch her.

"Uh, okay, Penelope. I don't think he's going anywhere for a while anyway, but I'll make sure he stays here. Why? What's up?"

"Dan Hughes is a possible witness in Doug's case," she told him.

And if he had been beaten up, Penelope could make a good guess about who had done it.

CHAPTER 27

PENELOPE PULLED HER cruiser into the parking lot of the clinic and went inside. Jacob met her with a big hug.

Not that it was unusual for her to hug her fiancé. But it felt good to find the time for it, finally. It was nearing seven o'clock now. The way the weekend had gone, they had barely seen each other.

"What's happening in this town, Penny?" he asked her.

"I'm working on it. Where is he?" she asked him. "Where's Dan Hughes?"

"Down in Exam Room Two," he told her. "Officer Ramirez is there with him, making sure he doesn't leave."

"How's his shoulder?" Penelope asked.

"His shoulder's fine. So is his attitude. And his physique...he's a good-looking guy and he knows it."

Jacob ran his hand through his hair as they started walking to the back of the clinic where the exam rooms were. "But he doesn't have my hair..."

"Or your fiancé," added Penelope.

"Anyway," Jacob said, motioning with his hand to the wood door with the number two on it. "They're in there. Aunt Jessie is going to be dropping Trevor off soon."

Penelope sighed. They still hadn't told Trevor that his mother had been murdered. How did you tell that to a five year old? No child should lose a parent at that age. Just as she'd lost both of hers at the tender age of eight, after their house burned to the ground.

"Hey, Penny?" Jacob said to her, squeezing her hand tighter. "You okay?"

She showed him a smile she didn't really feel. "Fine, baby. Just tired."

She watched him walk away, appreciating what God had brought into her life. Jacob was more than just a pretty face. He was her strength.

* * *

Officer Ramirez sat in a chair just inside the exam room door, his normally robust, light-brown complexion looking a little gray. His uniform shirt was off and folded on the floor next to him, and had been replaced with a simple white sleeveless t-shirt. A bandage covered his shoulder where Jacob had stitched him up. He smiled at

Penelope and hooked a thumb at the man lying on the room's padded bed.

"Dan Hughes," he said to her. "Although I don't think I needed to stay to watch over him. He's not going anywhere."

Penelope looked at the man, covered up to his chest with a crisp white sheet; his face a mixture of dark bruises. He breathed deeply through his open mouth, his nose puffy and swollen. One eye watched them both. The other was swollen shut.

"I'll take over, Anthony. Thank you," Penelope said. "How's your shoulder?"

"Hurts. Guess life in a small town isn't always quiet." He stood up and walked out of the room, closing the door behind him.

"Mr. Hughes. Dan?" Penelope said as she went and stood next to the bed. "I'm officer Chance. Can you talk to me for a minute?"

Dan nodded his head as best he could.

"Sir, you told the doctor that you fell down some stairs."

Dan wouldn't meet her eyes.

"I know you're a good church-going man. You didn't fall down any stairs, did you?"

The man hesitated, and then shook his head. "Told me...told me he...would hurt me...again if...I talked."

"Dear Lord, please help this man," Penelope prayed out loud. "I'm sure he didn't do anything to deserve what has happened to him. But I also know he has something he needs to tell me. Please help him. Thank You, Lord. Amen."

"Amen," echoed Dan. He reached out his hand with a pleading look on his face. When Penelope grasped it, the man closed his eyes, took an easier breath and sighed in obvious relief.

"Thank...you," Dan croaked.

Penelope wasn't sure what she was being thanked for, but she replied, "You're welcome."

"Have...something...to tell...you."

"Do you know who did this to you?"

He took a deep, shaky breath. "Not his...name. Know...his...face."

"Can you give me a description?" Penelope asked him.

"Hurts...to talk." He swallowed heavily, and his one eye looked over towards the table next to the bed, with its glass of water. Penelope reached over for it and held it for Dan, positioning the straw in such a way that he could drink.

"Okay. How about I ask the questions and you can nod if I'm right?"

Dan took a sip of water and nodded.

"So," Penelope began. "This happened because you saw something on Friday night?"

Dan nodded, pushing the straw away.

"Around Ricky's Pub?"

Another nod.

"Do you know who Doug Foster is?"

Another nod.

"Did what you saw have anything to do with Doug's truck?"

"Blue truck...with flames," he managed.

"Did you see someone drive it away from the bar?"

After a hesitation, Dan gave one, slow nod.

Penelope almost didn't want to ask this next question but she knew that she had to. "Was it Doug?"

To Penelope's relief, the answer was no.

"Was it the guy who did this to you?"

Dan swallowed and then managed to rasp, "Yes. He said...said he...saw me...Friday night...walking..."

"Walking your Pomeranian?"

"Yes...He was waiting...at my house...when I...came back...back from Jacksonville. He told me...to...keep... quiet..."

Penelope held the man's hand tightly again. "It's okay, Dan. It's all right. We're going to put him away for this. Can you tell me what you saw?"

Dan nodded. And when Dan had finished making his painful way through his story, a lot of the pieces finally fit.

CHAPTER 28

HEADING BACK TO the office, she had a feeling there would be something waiting for her. Turned out she wasn't wrong. Things were happening quickly now. Everything was starting to make sense and Penelope was beginning to be able to see the big picture, even if it was fuzzy around the edges. "God," she prayed as she drove into the station parking lot, "I thank you for your help so far. Please, let it continue in this way, so that the light of truth may shine, and innocent men will not face wrongful justice. Thank you, God."

When she got to her desk she found a thick manila envelope with her name and the station address on it. She knew what it was from the return address, and she ripped it open to find the evidence report from Doug's truck. Just a day earlier, she would have been afraid to look at it, afraid it would only give further proof that Doug was guilty of attempted murder. But now she knew better, and scanning through the trace evidence report, she found exactly what he was looking for.

She knew about the dents in the grille and on the hood, and the cracked headlight with blood on it. The blood was a match to Pete's. No surprises there. It was Doug's truck that ran down Pete.

It was the fingerprint evidence that was the big news.

"What's that?" asked Chief Jackson's deep voice.

Penelope looked up from the information in front of her with a smile. "The biggest piece of the puzzle yet, Chief." She handed over the whole packet and sat quietly while the Chief read through it.

The Chief whistled a note, low and long. "I would never have expected that!"

"My thoughts exactly, sir," Penelope said. "At least I wouldn't have, if I hadn't just spoken with Dan Hughes."

"Dan Hughes? Think I know him. Lives over near Ricky's Pub. Nice guy. Annoying dog."

Penelope smiled. "Yes, that's him. He gave me a description of a guy he saw drive away in Doug's pickup truck from the bar on Friday night, and the time frame puts it just before Pete Lamb was run down. That description matches the owner of those fingerprints on page four. If I may say so, I believe this exonerates our prime suspect. It means Doug is innocent."

"Now Penelope," the Chief said, "you know we need

more than this."

"More than fingerprints? More than an eye witness who got beat up for seeing what he saw?"

"Yes," the Chief said simply, sitting down in the chair next to Penelope's desk.

"What more could we possibly need, sir?" Penelope felt her anger rising and did her best to control it but it was just so frustrating, to be so close to setting Doug free, only to have the Chief throw up a roadblock.

"You have a witness who saw this guy in Doug's truck, and the fingerprint evidence proves that too. But, do you have someone who saw this guy try to kill Pete in Doug's truck?"

Penelope hated to admit it, but she had to. "No. I don't have that."

"Do you have a motive?" The Chief pressed.

"Well, kind of. It's all guess work at this point."

Chief Jackson just looked at Penelope, and said nothing else. Penelope slumped back in her chair. "Okay, fine. Let me finish up with our suspect, and I'll get what we need."

"You're sure of that?" The Chief tapped a finger on Penelope's desk.

"Yes. I think with this, I can get the truth from him. I'm confident I can."

The Chief nodded. "Good. That's what I like to hear, Penelope. I'm going to watch you finish the interview."

"Great. Let me gather a few notes and things and

I'll get at it. Do we have time of death from Gainesville M.E. yet?"

"Not yet."

"Our guy is still in the interrogation room?"

The Chief nodded. "Yes. Findley's just where you left him. He's not happy about it, but that's too bad."

Penelope nodded agreement. Findley had a lot to answer for.

Starting with why it was his fingerprints that were inside of Doug's truck.

CHAPTER 29

MICHAEL FINDLEY WAS still in the chair where Penelope had last seen him, handcuffed by each wrist to a chair arm. Penelope could tell that some of the bravado that had been in the man last time had evaporated. Some of it, but not all.

"You need anything, Mr. Findley?" she asked in a conversational tone as she sat down with her folder opposite the man. She started leafing through the papers as if she was trying to find something.

"I need to get out of here, is what I need," Findley answered her. "Why don't you just charge me for cutting that cop and bring me in front of a judge already?"

Penelope refused to rise to the bait. Her anger at Findley was justified, considering what she now knew, but anger wouldn't help her solve this puzzle. Findley still had information she needed. And God willing, the man was going to give it to Penelope. He just didn't know it yet.

"We're working up the charges on that right now, Mr. Findley. And the charges for breaking into the doctor's house." Her fiancé's house, but she wasn't about to tell Findley that. "So, let's talk about something else."

Findley shook the handcuffs against the metal chair. "Sure. Let's talk. I'm not going anywhere."

Penelope leaned back in her chair and dropped her pen on top of her folder. "You've been in here for a while. You need to use the bathroom? Drink water? There's a water cooler right over there in the corner."

Findley looked at her with a blank stare. "No, I'm good. Thanks. Let's just get on with this."

Penelope nodded. "Okay. I want to remind you that you've been read your Miranda rights, and also that we're still recording this interview. So I have some questions I want to ask you."

"Ask away, officer. I don't have anything to hide. I've told you everything, and I know that I'm going to jail when we're done. I got nothing to hide."

Penelope centered her thoughts and said a short prayer that God would guide her. This was the most important interview she'd done in a long time. And she knew exactly what question she would start with.

"How do you know Doug Foster?" she asked.

Findley blinked. It was just a simple little thing, but

it told Penelope she'd struck her target.

"He's my girlfriend's ex-husband," was the answer Findley finally gave. "Father of that kid of hers. That's all."

Penelope wrote it down on paper just like Findley said it. "Okay. So you've never met him before?"

"Nope. I came into town to see what kind of man he was. That was on Friday. I followed him just like I told you, to that pizza place, and to that bar, and then I watched him drive away. Then I watched him come back, and then he went to another bar, and I left him there. Simple."

"It actually is pretty simple, the way you lay it out," Penelope said to him. "Kind of as if you have it memorized."

"Not hard to remember it. It was only three days ago."

"And you're sure that's how it happened?"

The smile on Findley's face was infuriating. "Yup. Just like that."

"Okay. Okay good. I just wanted to get that down so that we were all on the same page, Mr. Findley. See, I had two things, before you came along, that told me Doug didn't actually run anyone over. Now I've got three."

"What are you talking about?"

Penelope settled her elbows on the flat surface of the metal table and counted out her points on her fingers. "See, first of all, I have faith. Faith in the skills and intelligence that God gave me, and everything in me was saying something was wrong with this case. That there was something I was missing. So I wasn't willing to just write Doug off when everything pointed at him. My faith told me to dig deeper. So that's one.

"Then, I managed to find some witnesses that backed up at least part of his story. That was two. Of course, your story, as you gave it, contradicted number two, so I was glad when I found number three."

"And what was number three, officer?" Findley asked with a sneer.

Penelope turned the folder in front of her around and pushed it across the table so that Findley could read it.

"That right there is a report on latent evidence found in Doug's truck which we seized from The Last Chance Tavern, where you said you left Doug. So, if all you did was follow Doug that night, Mr. Findley, and you've never met him before, I'm stumped. How did your fingerprints get into his truck?"

Findley's eyes narrowed. "No way. You're lying. Or someone is trying to set me up. You're trying to get me to trip myself up! That's all it is!"

Penelope shook her head at the man. She had him now. Finally that cool facade of his had cracked.

Gotcha.

"It's right there in the report. You can see it for yourself. Oh, you were so smart about it that the steering wheel had been wiped clean. But you kind of neglected everything else. You know the first thing people do when they get into a strange vehicle? They adjust the mirrors."

And there it was on Findley's face. He knew he'd been had.

"There's a nice set of your prints on the glass of the rearview mirror. Add into that the fact that you beat up a good man just to keep him quiet about seeing you driving Doug's truck, and guess what that means?"

Findley chewed on his lip and his eyes bored holes through the report in front of him.

"I know you weren't counting on Dan Hughes talking. You thought you'd put enough fear in him that he'd never say anything about seeing you that night. But he's a good Christian man and he knows that the truth is stronger than fear. And here's the truth. You were driving Doug's truck when it hit Pete, Mr. Findley. You tried to pin it on Doug. Maybe it was because Doug was going to take Camille away, like you said. But I have the feeling I'm missing something. What am I missing?"

Findley tried to reach out to the report but the chains on the handcuffs were too short. "Fine. I admit it. My prints are in his truck. It was me. Okay? I took Doug's truck for a little joyride and hit that guy. I figured that Doug was already drunk; he wouldn't even notice the damage it had done to his truck. And I was right! He came out of that bar so blitzed that he walked right by the front of his truck and didn't even see what had happened. Then, he drove to another bar! He did not deserve Camille! I deserved Camille. Me! She belonged to me!"

Penelope let the man rant. Let him say whatever he wanted to, knowing it was all being recorded. Let him hang himself. He stole Doug's truck, hit Pete and then he tried to pin it on Doug, Penelope's best friend in the world.

But it hadn't worked.

Thank you, Lord, Penelope thought. *I never should have doubted that you had a plan in all this.*

"Now, Mr. Findley," Penelope said, collecting the folder back, "let's talk about your whereabouts the rest of the weekend. Tell me why you killed Camille."

Penelope was surprised to actually see tears in the man's eyes. Was he crying because he'd been caught? Because he was so angry? Or did he actually have real feelings for Camille?

"You can't touch me on that one, officer," Findley snapped. "I didn't kill her. And I'm done talking to you."

With that, Findley slumped into his chair, and try as Penelope would, he didn't say another word.

CHAPTER 30

CHIEF JACKSON WAS smiling when Penelope came out of the interview room. "Nicely done, officer. That gets Doug off for the attempted murder of Pete. Very good job."

"Half a job, Chief. I got him to confess to trying to kill Pete. But not for killing Camille."

Jim Saunders was still there, watching Findley through the room's two-way mirror. "Don't know, Penelope. Seems to me this guy might be telling the truth."

Penelope took a deep breath and scrubbed at her face, and then ran her fingers through her blond hair. "I don't know, Jim. I just have a gut feeling that he did it. But I'm more convinced than ever that Doug didn't do it."

Chief Jackson put his hand on Penelope's shoulder. "We just have to find the proof."

"I know, sir. There's more to this puzzle yet. But, if I might say so, I think we can let Doug go now. I'll keep him under house arrest still, if you like."

The Chief looked at Penelope for a long moment. "He's still on the hook for Camille's murder, Penelope."

"There's not enough to charge him."

"Not enough to clear him, either," the Chief pointed out. "Unless you can pull some other miracle out of your hat."

"The only one who can do miracles is God, Chief. He's already pulled one here. I have a feeling He's got more in store for us."

"Okay. If you can promise he'll stay at your place, then I'll turn him over to your custody, so to speak. But he's got to keep his nose clean, Penelope. I'm taking a big risk with this."

Penelope nodded, happy she finally had some good news to give her friend.

"Officer Saunders," the Chief turned to Jim and pointed a finger at the man in the interview room, "book this piece of garbage and get him transported over to the County Correctional Facility. After that, take off and be with that wife of yours. I know you two need the extra money, with the baby coming, but I'm sure she needs her husband around now, too."

Jim smiled. "I'm sure she does, too, Chief. Thank you. Man, the list of charges we got on this guy! Aggravated assault on an officer, burglary, attempted murder! Then all the smaller stuff like auto theft. Did I miss anything?"

"Assault on Dan Hughes, the witness who saw him driving that night. Poor guy was in the wrong place at the wrong time."

"Or," the Chief said, "maybe the right place at the right time. Why don't you go have another talk with him, Penelope? Maybe something else will jog loose in his memory."

"I will, Chief. But I want to get Doug released first and back home. And I could use some sleep myself. This has been the longest weekend of my life. I'll go to the clinic first thing in the morning and talk with Dan again."

"That's fine," the Chief told her. "Longest weekend any of us have had in a long time, I'd wager."

Penelope helped Jim with some of the specifics of the charges against Michael Findley, and then went back to the holding cell. Doug was awake now and sitting up. He stared at the ceiling until he heard Penelope coming. "Penny?" he said, standing up and coming to the bars of the cell. "Penny, what's going on? I've been back here for I don't know how long. Where's Trevor? Is he okay? When can I see him? When can I get out?"

Penelope smiled and produced her key ring, with the key to the cell door on it. "I've got some good news for you, buddy. You ready to go home?"

CHAPTER 31

DINNER THAT MONDAY night at the Chance home was a joyous affair, a celebration over containers of take-out Chinese food. It was held later than usual, but no one minded. Doug sat with Trevor on his lap, letting his son taste egg rolls and sweet and sour chicken for the first time. Trevor made various faces with each one, only really interested in the fortune cookies. It felt good for Penelope to be out of her uniform for a change and enjoying the company of her friends.

And the company of her fiancé. She and Jacob hugged each other for a very long time, taking strength from their closeness. "Sorry I haven't been around much this weekend," she told him, still holding him close.

He shrugged as Penelope nuzzled into his shoulder. "I've chosen to marry a cop. I understand the risks."

"You sure they can spare you at the clinic?"

"Nurse Taylor has the night shift. I told her to call me if anything comes up. It's just Dan Hughes there now, and since you caught the man who assaulted him, I'm sure he's going to sleep a lot better."

"You'll be sleeping better too," she said to him, stroking his dark brown hair. "That guy, Findley, he's just bad. I don't know what happened to him to make him this way, but I can't find a single good thing about him. I'm glad we got him off the streets."

"Just sad it had to happen this way?"

She laughed softly. "You know me too well."

"I'd better, if you're going to become Mrs. Penelope Gordon," Jacob said with a wink and a smile.

She kissed him, longer and with more purpose than she ever had before. "Have I told you lately how much I love you?" she said when she finally broke away.

He was almost breathless, but managed to say, "I'm not sure. I think you have, but not like you did just now."

"Auntie Penny," Trevor said to her, crumbling a triangular piece of fortune cookie over his plate. "Where's mama?"

Silence filled the room as the whole world came crashing down. Penelope looked at Doug. There were tears in her friend's eyes.

"Penelope, Jacob, can you give Trevor and me a moment?" Doug asked them.

"Do you want us to stay, maybe?" Jacob offered.

Penelope could tell how his heart went out to Trevor.

"No, thank you though." Doug turned Trevor around and held him tightly. "I need to do this."

Penelope and Jacob walked outside, holding each other's hands. "I wish I could do this for him," Penelope admitted. "He's been there for me so often, and through so much."

He gave her hand a squeeze. "And you're here for him now."

She shrugged. "Yeah, I guess."

"But not like his family was there for you when you were younger?"

She swallowed and wouldn't look him in his eyes. "You know that's the one thing in my life I haven't talked to you about."

"Yes, you have," he said. "You've told me all about it."

But she shook her head. "I've told you the facts of what happened. Most of them. But I haven't really talked to you about it."

He touched her face lightly with his fingertips. "I just figured that when you were ready, you'd lay that down. I guess all of this has brought it back up for you, hasn't it?"

A nod was all she could manage. Visions of that night—so long ago, when her family's home burned down and left her orphaned, swam through her head. They were always there, just below the surface, never really going away. It was the one burden she had carried with her all these years, never being able to let it go. She had lived, while her parents had died.

It had been a lot for a girl of eight to handle. It still was a lot for her.

If Doug's parents hadn't taken her in and made her like their own daughter, she might never have grown up to be where she was now.

He hugged her again, and just held her. The tears started and he held her while she wept.

When she was finally able to draw a steady breath again she whispered, "Thank you."

"I love you back," he answered her.

Standing here, under a clear night sky, in the arms of the man she loved, she knew that God had truly blessed her.

"You need to lay this down completely, Penelope," he said to her. "You need to give it over to God and let it be laid to rest. I love you, for everything you are. But you've got a lot of room inside of you being taken up by this tragedy. Don't let it weigh you down anymore."

She knew he was right. She also knew that the reason she hadn't committed to a wedding date yet was this baggage she carried. And she thought that now, with him here, she was more ready than she had ever been to get rid of it. Just not quite yet.

"I will," she assured him. "But Doug needs me first. When everything's done with him, I'll try healing myself. I promise."

He laid a hand over her heart. "You can't heal yourself,

silly. Only God can do that for you."

They kissed again. When they stepped apart, she knew he was getting ready to go home. "You could stay the night, if you want," she said to him. "You or Doug could take the couch."

"I'm going to go home tonight. There's a lot of temptation here. And you and I will have the rest of our lives to sleep under one roof soon enough."

She walked him to his car and kissed his cheek as he got in.

"Tell Doug I said I'm happy for him," he said, and then he was driving away down the street.

Penelope couldn't wait for the day when they would be married. Having that kind of love and encouragement in her life meant a lot to her. It was the first time she had felt truly loved, unconditionally loved, since her parents' deaths. Doug and his family had done their best for her, and she had grown to love them like the surrogate family they had been. But it wasn't the same.

With Jacob, she'd found something that was missing in her life. And it might finally be enough for her to let go of the dead weight of a child's pain she had carried with her all these years.

The sound of the door to her house closing interrupted her memories. Turning, she saw Doug stepping out, his eyes red in the dim porch lights. He sat down on one of the folding chairs Penelope had set up there and hung his head.

Penelope sat down next to him. "You put Trevor to bed?"

Doug nodded. "That poor kid. I told him that his mother went to Heaven, and tried to answer everything for him the best I could. He cried a little, but then you know what he said to me? He says, "That's okay daddy, we'll be with her in Heaven one day.""

Penelope had to smile at that. She couldn't help herself. The things that a child said often put grown-up worries into perspective. "I'm sorry, Doug. I really am. Is there anything I can do for you?"

Doug pushed his hands over his short hair. "Well, I could really use a beer right now."

Penelope shook her head.

"I know, I know. I want one, really badly Penny, but I'm not going to. Not so long as Trevor's here. I owe him that much."

They sat in silence for a while, staring out at the night.

"You have to get this guy for me, Penny," Doug said to her after a long time.

"I will, buddy. God willing, I will."

"You talk to Pete again? Tell him it wasn't me?"

"Pete's still at Grace Memorial. I'll have Jacob check on him tomorrow. For tonight, let's just get some rest. The both of us have earned it, I think."

"Amen, sister."

Hearing him call her that again brought a tired smile to her lips.

Even so, even as tired as they were, they stayed on the porch a while longer, just taking comfort from each other's company.

CHAPTER 32

THAT TUESDAY MORNING was the first time Penelope had considered calling in sick when she wasn't. Her body was still exhausted when the alarm went off at seven in the morning. Her eyes blinked repeatedly in an attempt to focus. She yawned over and over.

And if her best friend's good name wasn't still on the line, then she might just have allowed herself to tell that little white lie and stay home, pretending to be sick. But Doug wasn't out of the woods yet. And it was up to her to make sure the truth got found out.

It was pretty clear at this point that Doug didn't kill his ex-wife. Penelope had already cleared him of the attempted murder of Pete, but being able to show Doug probably didn't kill Camille wouldn't be enough to clear him in the minds of everyone in town. And Penelope felt she owed it to Doug to not only clear his name in the criminal courts, but in the hearts of his neighbors as well. So she struggled out of bed, showered, and dressed in her uniform for work. After a quick bite of toast with jam, she got up from the kitchen table and headed for the door.

And on the way out, the phone rang.

"I swear, I'm going to disconnect this thing," she mumbled to herself. The caller ID showed the call came from the Franklin Clinic.

She picked up the receiver. "Jacob?" she guessed.

"Hey, officer beautiful," Jacob greeted her. "Got some good news for you."

"Mmm. Good news, brought to me by a handsome man. What a way to start my day!"

He laughed. "Pete is being released from Grace Memorial this morning."

"Oh, yeah?" That was good news.

"Yup. Got the call half an hour ago. Woke me out of a sound sleep, too."

"Yeah, I know the feeling."

"He's going to be in a lot of pain for a long time, but he's good to go outpatient now, according to the doctors over there. It's been four days now, after all."

Penelope counted on her fingers. He was right. Today marked the fourth day since the attack on Pete. "So how's he getting home, then?"

"From what I understand," Jacob told her, "his sister

is going to pick him up. I'm guessing you can talk to him at her house later today. And I'm going to stop by there later too. Not that I don't trust the doctors over at Grace Memorial, but I'd kind of like to examine him myself, just to be sure."

Penelope chuckled. "That's my man."

"Yes. I am." She could hear the smile in his voice. "Want to show me how much you love me tonight? Maybe, with dinner?"

"That sounds great. You pick the place. I'll pick you up around six, okay? You over at the clinic now?"

"Yep. Am I going to see you?"

"I need to speak to Dan Hughes again. The Chief wants to know if he remembers anything else, so I guess I'll see you there."

"I'll be waiting," he said. "Love you."

"Love you back." She hung up and left for work, letting Doug and Trevor sleep in. They both needed it.

* * *

Penelope radioed Dispatch and let them know she wouldn't be coming straight into the office. She turned her car toward the clinic. She saw Jacob's car already at the clinic when she arrived. He was waiting for her at the door.

"Good morning," He leaned in to her as they embraced. "Dan Hughes is awake and he's asking for you already. How about that?"

"Is he okay to talk to me?"

He nodded, stepping back from her and leading her by the hand. "He's stronger today than yesterday. But still, don't overtax him."

Dan started to speak the moment she entered the room. His bruises looked worse. "I need to speak to you," he said in a raspy voice. "I promise not to talk much."

Now he had Penelope's interest and curiosity. "Okay, but only for a minute or two," she said.

Dan nodded and smiled as best he could, reaching for Penelope's hand and taking hold of it.

"I understand that it comforts you, Dan," Penelope said, "but I have a feeling there's another reason you insist on holding my hand when I'm around. Am I right?"

"That's what I wanted to tell you officer," Dan said, swallowing. "First, you need to understand. I'm not a freak or anything." It was obvious to Penelope how much pain the man was in. One more good reason for Michael Findley to spend the rest of his days behind bars. "Each of us has...a special gift. From God. Me, you, everyone. I can...feel the truth about a person. By touching them."

Penelope thought maybe that Dan had suffered a concussion, and it must have shown on her face.

"Need you...to believe me, officer." Dan said, his expression pleading.

"You can tell these things about everyone you touch?" Penelope asked.

"No," Dan admitted. "Only certain people. Only some of the time. But what I find out...from my gift. It's never wrong."

"So that's why you grab onto my hand?"

"That's part of it," Dan said, trying to sit up more. "But with you there's...something else. Your faith. I can feel your faith. It gives me strength...comfort. And hope."

"I'm not sure I understand what you mean," Penelope said.

"Your faith in God is strong," Dan said, more clearly than he'd said anything else. "It...powers you. No. I mean motivates you. To do what's right. Because of that, you will conquer the evil...of the man who hurt you...who has been hurting the folks of this town."

Penelope was dumbfounded. "I appreciate what you're saying, but we both know it's up to God to conquer evil. We're just His instruments."

Dan nodded, and smiled with puffy lips. "Exactly, officer. You are His instrument. His laborer here. On Earth. But, there's...one more thing. When I touch your hand I can tell you still carry the weight with you. Of that day. I was here, when your parents died. I was here... in Franklin. I know how horrible that was. For you. You can't keep that pain. Not...yours. Give it back."

The conversation she'd had with Jacob just last night, and all the memories of that bad night that had resurfaced this weekend, all came back at her in a rush. And to her surprise, tears began to run down her cheeks again. Emotion from events, both in the past and the present, stirred in her uneasily. "I don't know how," she said.

"Just entrust it to the one who can comfort you, Penelope," Dan said. "That's all you need...to do."

Penelope didn't know what to make of Dan's words, or his assertion of a special gift from God. But she knew that what Dan said was true. As Jacob had told her last night, she'd carried this long enough. It was time to let it go. Somehow. When everything else was settled. Wiping her face with her free hand, Penelope smiled and said, "Okay, enough talking for now. You need to rest your voice for a while."

Dan blinked at her. "You had...questions?"

"The Chief wanted me to ask you if you remembered anything else about Friday night."

Dan nodded and began to talk. Penelope took notes.

CHAPTER 33

THIS DIDN'T MAKE any sense.

She read through her notes from her talk with Dan Hughes four times. She'd shown them to Jacob, and he was just as baffled as she was. And now, she was riding around Franklin, driving to clear her head.

Franklin was actually a very old town, as towns in Florida went. Some of the buildings dated back to the 1820s. The town still had its original street layout, even though it had changed a bit over the years and of course become more modern. Florida hadn't become a state until 1845, the last state east of the Mississippi River. But there had been people living here before then, and in the cemetery on the outskirts of town were any number of headstones with faded dates from the 1700s. She'd always loved to go exploring in that cemetery when she was a kid. That was before her parents had died and been buried there. She hadn't been back since.

Now, she found herself driving there.

Penelope parked her car just inside the open gate of Meadowvale Cemetery and stepped out under the shade of a huge Persimmon tree. It was a beautiful place, full of flowers and well maintained shrubbery. She still remembered where the graves were. Side by side, with stones her grandparents had picked out. She found the graves and knelt between them, facing the headstones.

She didn't know what to say. She'd thought of her parents almost every day since their deaths, had wished them alive again and prayed that God might bring them back more times than she could count. Then, in her adult years, they had been a constant reminder in the back of her head to do what was right, because life was too short.

But now that she was here, with the intention of speaking to them again, of talking it out and laying down her burden, she had no idea how to even start.

"Mom, Dad," she finally began, "I'm sorry I haven't come back before now. It just hurt me so much to be reminded of your deaths. I guess I was trying to run away from the pain." She was surprised to hear herself laugh. "Not that it worked. It still hurts. Every day. But I don't want it to hurt anymore. I don't want to be sad about this for the rest of my life. I don't want to forget you. Ever. But I need to let go of this. You understand, I'm sure. And God, I know that You understand and will help me and take this away."

The memory flashed through her mind again. The house on fire. Her parents running with her to the door.

She jolted, feeling something inside her crack a little. The pain flooded up and she took in a deep breath and kept going. "I'm going to be married soon, Mom, Dad. I know it's hard for me to believe too. You'd like him. He's a wonderful man. My rock. My strength. I don't know what I'd do without him."

The fire was too hot, too big, it was everywhere, and they couldn't get out.

"Uh, uh, I know what happened that night, guys. I remember everything. And it hurts, still. Maybe it shouldn't, but it does."

Her mom, lifting her up and out of the kitchen window. "Run, baby, run away. Fast as you can, now. Go!"

The crack widened, and something, some force or pressure, bled out from it, seeped out and lifted away.

And the fire whooshed up behind her as she got out. And her parents didn't make it. And she stood there on that front lawn calling for them until the fire trucks arrived and someone took her in their arms and carried her away.

"I just wish you hadn't died. I love you Mom. I love you Dad."

She wept. Hot tears trickled down her cheeks, that burned as they came out but then cooled as they evaporated off her face. The pain lifted from her, an aching sorrow so ingrained in her that she hadn't even realized how deeply it ran, until now. And when the tears stopped, the pain was with her no longer.

She touched each gravestone in turn, tracing the names of her parents. "Thank you, God, for this moment. For the memory of love that I can take away with me in place of the guilt I had been carrying. I lay that down now God, and ask for the strength to walk away from it and let it go."

Penelope Chance stood up, feeling lighter than she had, somehow feeling stronger and more...alive.

CHAPTER 34

PENELOPE WAS BACK at the police station before ten that morning. The Chief was in the office talking something over with Saunders, back for another shift himself after taking the night off. Chief Jackson saw Penelope come in and walked over to her just as Penelope sat down at her desk.

"You were over speaking to our witness, Dan Hughes, I'm guessing?" he asked Penelope.

"Yes, sir. I spoke with him. I had one errand to run on the way back or I'd have been here a bit earlier. Sorry. I can promise you it was necessary, though."

The Chief waved a hand. "I'm not concerned about it. With all the extra time you've been putting in around here, I wouldn't have been surprised if you asked for a personal day. I can spare you a little time for an errand.

But tell me what Hughes had to say."

"I've got his statement right here, sir," Penelope said to him. " And I can tell you up front, I don't know what to make of it."

Penelope handed him the notepad she had used to write out his answer to the simple question, *did you see Pete Lamb that night?* At least, Penelope had thought it was a simple question. It turned out to be anything but.

The Chief read through the three page statement. "He's sure about this?"

"Yes."

"Well," the Chief mused. "Now that we know what he saw, what does it mean?"

"It means more headache for us. For me, in particular. Pete got released from Grace Memorial Hospital this morning. I'm going to go over to his house a little later and talk to him. Maybe he has some explanation for this."

"He got released? Seriously? I thought his injuries were pretty bad," the Chief said as he handed the notepad back to Penelope.

"They were. Bad enough for a three-day stay in Grace Memorial, anyway. They say he's good enough now for outpatient, so they must have fixed him up. I'll see when I get out there. What happened with our boy Findley?"

Chief Jackson sat down and stretched his legs out in front of him. "Nothing much. Saunders got the paperwork done up for an arraignment, and Judge Dirksen put him in jail without bail. Findley actually laughed when Dirksen signed the order of remand." He shook his head. "That man troubles me. It's not often we deal with someone that you can classify as actually evil, but he comes as close as I've ever seen."

"That he does. Makes you wonder what he's capable of."

"Well, I'd say it's a safe bet he's capable of killing his girlfriend, wouldn't you?" the Chief raised an eyebrow as he asked the question.

Before Penelope could answer, the phone rang.

Saunders was busy, and when Penelope looked at the Chief, he just waved a hand. "Go ahead, answer it. We can talk more after."

Penelope picked it up on the fourth ring. "Franklin Police station. This is officer Chance."

"Penelope...help me," a woman's voice whispered.

Penelope stood up, pushing the chair out of the way as she did. "Who is this?" she asked.

"Patty Lamb," she answered. "Penelope, please help me. I'm here at the house with him. I don't know what he's going to do."

"He? Who, Patty? What who's going to do?"

The line went almost silent, but Penelope could still hear her labored breathing. "Patty, is it safe for you to talk?"

"No," came the whispered reply.

"Patty, hold on. I'm on my way. Find some place safe in the house, and you stay there, you got it?"

As she was hanging up the phone, she heard Patty whisper, "Hurry!"

"What was that all about?" the Chief asked her.

"Patty Lamb. Pete's sister. She's in trouble. It sounds like someone's in her house. Saunders!" she called over to Jim. "Get in a cruiser and follow me, we've got something going on over at the Lamb's house."

"Get out there quick, Penelope," the Chief told her, standing up and heading for his office. "I'll call over to the Florida Highway Patrol and see what they can give us for backup. Keep me posted."

Penelope was already out the door.

CHAPTER 35

PENELOPE WAS BEGINNING to wonder what else could possibly happen in the little Florida town of Franklin as she and officer Jim Saunders raced down the streets in their cruisers to the home of Pete and his sister Patty.

Penelope headed east on Main Street until it ended, and then turned left on Country Road towards Patty's house. Half a mile later, just past where Pete had been run over by Michael Findley using Doug's truck, she pulled into the driveway and turned the cruiser's engine off.

Jim was only a few seconds behind. They had shut the sirens off back in town, after they had cleared traffic, so that whoever was here with Patty wouldn't have advance warning they were coming. But they were here now, and no hiding it. She surveyed the house.

House was kind of a generous term. Patty and Pete lived in a rundown cracker-style home that had seen better days. The board siding was falling off in some places and the tin roof was curling at the edges. Penelope had been in the place before, and so she knew that Patty kept it neat and tidy inside, but she also knew that Pete's drinking had kept them from having a lot of the money it would have taken to fix the place up.

"Jim," she said quietly as Saunders came up to her, "see if you can get around back—keep out of sight, and just make sure no one comes out that isn't me or Patty. When the Highway Patrol gets here, brief them and station them outside and then you come in too. Okay?"

Jim nodded and was off around back.

Penelope drew her Sigma from its holster, just in case she needed it. She didn't like guns. Never had. And she had yet to solve any problem with one. But, not knowing what she was heading into, she wouldn't be doing herself or anyone else any favors by not being prepared. She entered the home carefully, pushing the door open with the barrel of her weapon, and then sweeping it from side to side as she sidestepped down the hallway.

The first room she came to was the home's kitchen. It had been built with a low wall dividing the dining area and the living room. Behind that wall, she found Patty, crouching down and holding the phone tightly to her chest.

"Penelope," she said. "Oh, thank God. He's in the

bedroom."

Penelope put a finger to her mouth to ask Patty to speak quieter, and then waved her over. She came, hesitantly, watching past the living room the whole time, down the hall where the bedrooms were.

When Patty reached her, Penelope leaned in close to her. "Patty, I have another officer outside. Jim Saunders. You know him. He's around back. I want you to go out to him, and let him know that you're okay. All right? Tell him I said to have you stay out by the patrol cars. Can you do that?"

She nodded, her whole body trembling. Whatever had happened had shaken her badly.

"You're not—" she started, but then swallowed and lowered her voice. "You're not going to hurt him, are you?"

"Patty, hurt who? Who's in here with you?"

She looked at Penelope as though she should already know. "Pete," she said. "It's Pete. My brother."

CHAPTER 36

"PATTY, WHAT'S GOING on? I thought Pete was just released from the hospital?"

"He was, Penelope. When we got home he started drinking. I begged him not to drink, Penelope, I begged him...And then he started going on about how he had messed things up and made all the wrong choices and then he got Daddy's rifle out—"

"Whoa," Penelope stopped her there. "Pete's got a rifle with him?"

Patty nodded, wide eyed.

"Is it loaded?"

She nodded again, her eyes terrified.

"Okay, Patty. It's going to be all right. Just go out to officer Saunders as I told you to, and make sure you tell him about the rifle, okay?"

"But Penelope, what are you going to do?" she asked.

"Everything I can, Patty. Go, now."

Patty set the phone down on the floor and crept out the back door.

"Dear Lord," Penelope prayed now. "Help me. Help me, and help Pete. I know there's more to what happened to him than anyone yet realizes, Lord God, but he doesn't need to do this. Please, help him realize that."

Moving in a sliding step, bringing her back foot up to her front foot, then stepping forward, back foot up to front again, just like her training had taught her to do, Penelope kept her pistol out and at low ready. Her throat was dry, and she could feel beads of sweat at the back of her neck. She could count on one hand the number of times she'd had to draw her gun in the line of duty. And never once had she done it with a friend involved.

"Pete?" she called out. No answer. "Pete, its Penelope. Penelope Chance. Can you come out of the bedroom and talk to me?"

"I'm on th' phone!" she finally heard Pete say in a shaky voice. "Don't you come in here!"

Penelope centered on the sound of Pete's voice. He was in the last room down on the left, which Penelope knew was Pete's bedroom. It had a single window that opened on the roadside of the building, away from where she had stationed Jim, and no other way out.

And the door was closed.

Okay, Penelope thought. So now what?

"Pete. Talk to me, Pete."

"I told you," Pete yelled at her. "I'm on th' phone!"

Penelope closed her eyes and asked God for protection. What she was about to do was probably foolhardy. But to save her friend, there might not be any other way.

Holding her gun low, she bladed her body to the door and opened it with her left hand. "Pete, I'm coming in."

"Stay out, Penelope!"

"I can't do that Pete. You know I can't. I'm going to come in, and we're going to talk. Patty said you have a gun in there. Do you have a gun in there?"

No answer. Penelope could hear Pete in there, talking in a low voice. And then, silence.

"Pete?"

The door swung open wider and Pete limped his way out. Penelope noticed several things at once, including the cast on Pete's right forearm, the yellowing bruises on his face, and the rifle held in his left hand.

Penelope took two steps back, but kept her gun low. "Pete. Put the gun down."

"Not yet," he said. Penelope could smell the liquor from where she stood and hear the slur in his words.

"Why not yet, Pete? Now seems like a great time for it in my book."

Pete shook his head and actually raised the rifle's end a little. "I'm waitin' on someone. You wanna wait with me? Do you Penelope?"

This wasn't getting them anywhere. If she kept

threatening Pete with her gun, Pete would stay defensive about holding on to his. Either way, this would be a stalemate. So she figured it was up to her to make the first move.

Slowly she holstered her gun and held her hands up. "Okay, Pete. Okay. Let's talk now. Let's just talk. What's going on here, Pete? Huh? Talk to me."

Pete lowered the rifle, but still held onto it. He shook his head and tried to rub at his eyes that were suddenly running with tears, but his cast wouldn't let him. "I screwed up, Penelope. Screwed up bad."

"I know, Pete. I know. You accused Doug of running you down. It wasn't him. We figured out who it was. The guy's in jail now and we cleared Doug. It's okay now, Pete."

But Pete was shaking his head even before Penelope was done speaking.

"Not that, Penelope! Th' other thing."

Other thing? "Pete, what are you talking about? Talk to me, buddy."

"I'm a drunk, Penelope. Always been a drunk. Screwed things up. Made a bad...bad mistake."

Penelope dared to take another step back toward Pete, keeping her eyes on the rifle. If she could get close enough, she knew she could get it away from him.

"Pete," Penelope tried again, "can you tell me what happened?"

Pete shook his head. "Can't. I did somethin'...I'm

a drunk. I owed...money. A lotta money. Patty doesn't know but they were gonna take the house...He said he'd pay me...pay me money."

Penelope took another step forward while Pete was distracted.

"All I wanted," Pete was saying, still trying to rub at his eyes, "was to get money for Patty. She's been so good t' me, Penelope. Been better t' me than I deserved. I just wanted t' help her, Penelope."

Penelope was becoming honestly worried about her friend. Something was not right. Pete was talking about something even worse than what Penelope herself suspected, and Penelope suspected a lot at this point. *God, help Pete lay this burden down, just as you helped me get rid of my own burden. Help him now, God, please.*

"Pete," she asked. "What did you do?"

Pete sobbed, tears choking his voice. "Don't matter, Penelope." He lifted the rifle.

"Pete, no!" Penelope cried out and stepped forward.

"Don't matter Penelope."

Everything stopped for a moment. The whole world came to a slow halt as Pete raised the rifle up and Penelope reached for it. She prayed harder than she had in a long time.

And then a familiar voice broke the stillness.

"Pete, I'm here."

Penelope stopped mid stride and turned around.

Doug stood in the hallway behind them.

"It's okay, Pete," Doug said. "I forgive you."

Penelope held her breath. She didn't know how Doug had gotten here, or how he'd gotten inside for that matter with officer Saunders outside, but she understood enough to know that Doug being there had stopped Pete from doing something drastic.

"Doug?" Penelope said, a world of questions in her voice.

"It's all right, Penny. I've got this." Doug stepped down the hallway until he was just a step or two in front of Penelope, within reach of Pete. "Put the gun down, Pete."

"Doug," Pete wailed, still sobbing. "You shouldn't've come. Not now. Told you on th' phone. I'm sorry, Doug, I'm so sososo sorry."

"I know, Pete. I know you are. It's done now. It's over. Please, Pete, give me the rifle."

Pete took a few shaky breaths and looked as though he might actually hand the gun over to Doug, but then gripped it tightly again, shaking his head. "No. Can't. I hav' to do this."

"No, Pete, you don't," Doug told him. "Me and Penelope and Patty and everyone cares for you. We're all here. We're here for you."

Penelope kept silent through the whole exchange, but kept herself ready to spring forward, to grab Doug, to grab the gun, to do whatever was necessary to end this. And at the same time she prayed that all that was needed to end this was just the gentle words that Doug was using.

"How can you fo'give me, Doug?" Pete asked, his hands shaking now. "You know wh' I did. I told you. On th' phone. Told you wh' I did."

So that was who Pete had been on the phone with when Penelope got in the house! Penelope thought it through. That still didn't explain what they were...

...oh, God help us. Everything was clicking into place for Penelope at that point. More pieces of the puzzle fell into place. But something still wasn't right.

She just didn't know what.

"I do forgive you, Pete," Doug was saying. "Because I'm your friend. Everything else, let's leave up to God. Okay? You can do that, right?"

Pete was silent, his hand still on the rifle. But slowly, he nodded.

Outside, sirens wailed as more police arrived. "That would be the Florida Highway Patrol coming in," Penelope explained. "Pete, don't worry about them. They'll stay outside. In here, it's just us friends, like Doug said. It's just us. Okay?"

"She's right, Pete," Doug said, reaching out his hand slowly. "Now, please, Pete, give me the gun."

To Penelope's amazement, Pete let Doug take hold of the rifle's barrel and pull it away from him.

Doug handed the gun back to Penelope and then he grabbed hold of Pete just as the man collapsed. Doug held Pete in his arms, letting him cry and wail and blabber incoherently.

Penelope took the gun back to the living room and unloaded it. One round in the chamber. Just one. But it would have been all that was needed to end Pete's life.

"Thank you, God," Penelope said out loud. "I don't know how you managed to let Doug intervene in this, but without his help, without Your help, it all would have ended badly. Thank you, God."

Doug was walking out of the hallway with Pete still holding tightly to him. Penelope pocketed the one bullet and made the rifle safe. "Okay," she said. "Let's get everyone out of here and down to the station." From her belt she unclipped her radio and keyed an open channel. "Jim, it's Penelope. I have Pete. We're all safe. And we're coming out the front."

Pete was done crying now, and just held onto Doug, breathing heavily. Together, Penelope and Doug walked him to the front door and then outside and down the front steps. There were three Highway Patrol units there, brownish-gray uniforms on, the officers from each standing behind their cruisers for cover, guns drawn.

"It's okay, guys, it's done," Penelope called out to them. "Situation clear." The officers seemed to relax a little, enough to put their guns away, at least, but did not move from position.

They put Pete in the back of Penelope's cruiser, behind the cage. When Penelope closed the door on him, she turned to Doug. Doug's face was an unreadable mask, but Penelope could see the pain in her friend's eyes.

"That was pretty brave, what you did in there, Doug," she told him, meaning every word.

Doug swallowed and nodded his head. "You have no idea how much it took for me to say those words to him. To say that I forgive him."

"I think I do." Penelope put a hand on his shoulder and let it rest there. "Did you mean them?"

Doug thought about it for a moment. "I think I did. At least, given enough time, I will mean them."

"Good. I know what it is to carry anger around for that long. It's not good for anyone."

"Can we, maybe, talk about this more down at the station? Or maybe after all this is done?"

"Of course, buddy. Of course." Penelope hugged Doug closely. "What did he tell you on the phone?"

Doug managed to whisper. "Said he killed Camille."

CHAPTER 37

THE MOOD IN the Franklin Police station was somber and quiet. Pete was in the interview room, handcuffed to the same chair that Michael Findley had been in the previous day. Doug and Penelope watched him through the two-way mirror as he slumped forward onto the interview room table, fast asleep, his body working off all the alcohol he had put into it.

"Tell it to me again. He called you on the phone, and told you what?"

Doug sighed and told the same story for the third time. "He told me that he had killed Camille. He said he hadn't wanted to do it, that he'd gotten himself roaring drunk to even think about doing it, and that he didn't remember a whole lot about it because he was so drunk."

"Okay. Doug, think real hard. What were his exact

words to you?"

Doug closed his eyes, replaying the conversation with Pete in his mind. "He said, 'Doug, I'm sorry, I was drunk,' and he said he didn't mean to do it, and then he said he got Camille killed."

Penelope latched onto that single important word. "He said he got Camille killed? Not, 'I killed her, but got Camille killed?'"

"Well, yeah, now that I'm talking about it with you, that's the word he used..."

"So he didn't do it?"

Doug stared at Penelope, his mouth open. "What are you saying? Penny, he confessed!"

"Doug, think about it for a moment...Camille dropped Trevor off on Saturday, right?"

"Well, yeah..."

"And Pete was run down by Findley Friday night."

"Yeah. So?"

"Well Pete was at Grace Memorial all weekend. He couldn't have killed Camille. What motive would he have anyway?" she asked.

"He told me he needed the money." He shook his head. "It's not a good reason. In fact, it's a lousy reason. But is there ever a good reason to kill anyone?"

"No," Penelope answered immediately. "No, there's not. Let me worry about the rest of it, Doug. There's something else you should know, and maybe that will make this a little clearer for you. Give you just a little bit of peace. Maybe."

"What's that?"

Penelope leaned her shoulder against the wall. "I talked with a witness. Dan Hughes is the guy's name. Says he knows you."

"Uh, yeah. Yeah, I think so. I did some work for him on his house. A little extra work to tide me over on some bills. Nice guy, if I remember. Noisy little dog."

"Yes, that's the guy. He saw Pete on Friday. At Ricky's Pub."

"Ricky's Pub?" Doug's eyes went wide. "That's where I was. But, Penelope, I don't remember seeing Pete there."

"You wouldn't have, buddy," Penelope told him. "Dan Hughes saw Pete outside. Talking to the guy who took your truck. Same guy who ended up running Pete down."

Doug blinked. Then blinked again. "Michael Findley? Pete was talking to Michael Findley? Why?"

"That's the question. But Dan said the two of them obviously knew each other. Findley beat Dan up because Dan saw them talking. *Arguing*, was actually how Dan put it. He wanted to keep Dan quiet about what he saw. Quiet about Findley driving your truck, but more than that. He wanted him to stay quiet about seeing Findley and Pete talking. It almost worked, too."

"So what Pete said...about Camille—" Doug had to take a second to draw a breath as he said his ex-wife's name. "All that had something to do with Findley."

"Looks like," was all Penelope said.

"Well, I don't know if that makes me feel better or not, but it's something. But how did Findley manage to take my truck? I mean, the keys were on me."

"Camille ever used your truck?" Penelope asked Doug.

"Well, yeah, I mean, back when we were married..." Doug caught on a second later. "She still had a key."

Penelope nodded. Pieces of the puzzle had started to fit in everywhere. "Let's sit down, Doug. You want some coffee?"

But Doug shook his head. "I need to get back to Trevor. I left him at the clinic with Jacob, and he was happy to see him and he was playing and all when I left, but he's still so sad. It will take him a long time to get used to the fact that his mother isn't coming back."

Penelope wanted to say something encouraging. Something reassuring. But nothing would come to her. There was nothing that would make this better.

Doug surprised her by taking hold of her hand. "Penelope, pray with me. Would you? I could really use it."

"Of course," she told her friend. They bowed their heads together.

"Lord God," Doug said, "thank You for my friend. Thank You for Penelope. Thank You for giving her the strength to see this terrible mess through. It's been...hard on me, God, and I ask You to stay with me and Trevor through the next little while, to help us through this. And please, stay with Penelope until this is done. There's more she has to do yet, and I wouldn't wish this on anyone alone. Together with You, she will be strong enough. As will we all. Amen."

"Amen," Penelope repeated. "Thank you, Doug. I needed that. I really did."

"No, Penelope. Thank you. I'll see you back at your place later."

"You will. Hey," Penelope said suddenly, "tell Jacob something for me?"

"You're not going to make me kiss him, are you?"

Penelope laughed. It was good to see Doug joke, after all that he'd been through in so few days. "No, I won't make you kiss him. But tell him I love him, and I laid it down. He'll know what you mean."

Doug's smile said a lot. "I know what you mean too, Penelope. And I'm glad to know it."

After Doug left the station, Penelope got ready for her interview with Pete.

CHAPTER 38

IT TOOK A little doing, but Penelope finally managed to get Pete awake again and sitting up. Her one-time friend's eyes were red and puffy from crying and from alcohol withdrawal. His hands shook almost nonstop. "You look like something the cat dragged in," Penelope said to him.

"I feel like something the devil used up and tossed aside, that is what I feel like," Pete answered, his words still thick. "I really do. I don't want to say the Devil made me do it, because he didn't. It was all me. My fault, no one else's. But I swear to you it's like something truly evil took over my thinking and I couldn't help myself."

Pete took a shaky, sucking breath, and stopped himself with an effort. Penelope was already taking notes. "Pete, I haven't read you your rights yet. I want to ask you some questions, but I need it all to be legal, okay?"

"I'll answer anything you ask me. I just want this over. I just want it off my chest. I want," another breath, "I want it all to stop."

"Okay, Pete. Okay. You and me, we'll get this over with. Soon, I promise."

"You mad at me, Penelope?"

The question took Penelope by surprise. "Mad? You're worried that I'm mad at you?" Penelope tried to wrap her mind around it. "Camille is dead, Pete. She was someone I knew. Someone Jacob and I both knew. And, you lied about Doug running you over. And you're worried that I'm mad at you?"

Pete nodded his head. "You're mad at me."

Penelope shook her head and tried to get his interview back on track. "Pete, try to focus for me, okay? I'm going to read you your rights, then I'm going to ask you my questions—you'll tell me what you know, and then you'll finally be able to get it all off your chest. How does that sound?"

"Fine," he said. "It don't matter no more anyway."

She read him his Miranda rights.

Before she could finish Pete started talking and crying at the same time. "I was done, Penelope. I'm a drunk, a no good drunk and everybody knows it. And sometimes I like to play cards, only I'm no damn good at it because of the drink. I drank and gambled up all my money and was drinking and gambling up all of Patty's too. She's a good woman... She's too good. She deserves better than a brother like me...She knew I was in her bank account. She knew where the money was going. Why didn't she stop me, Penny? Why?"

Penelope had no answer. She let him sit for a moment.

"They were gonna take the house. It ain't worth anything like it is, but they were gonna take it anyway. Still are, I guess. So I was gonna end it. I had Daddy's rifle and I was gonna end it. But I needed one more drink, you know? So then this guy came and told me he'd pay me fifty thousand dollars if I'd kill his girlfriend. Said he'd pay me half then, and half after the job...it sounded like a way out. I took that money, and I went to the apartment in Gainesville where this guy told me to go. I went there Friday afternoon like he told me to. Said he'd be over here in Franklin and nobody would know it was he who wanted his girl dead because he wouldn't be anywhere around."

"I didn't even know who his girl was until I got there. Then, when I got there and rang the bell and heard Camille's voice, I knew. I knew her. I knew she was Doug's ex. I couldn't do it. You know, I don't think I could have done it anyway? But when I heard it was Camille, I panicked and I ran and I drove back to Franklin and I told him. I told him I wasn't going to do it."

"That was when you met with Michael Findley at Rickey's Pub."

Pete nodded. "Didn't know his name. He was just the

guy with the money."

"Okay, but you met with the guy who paid you."

"Yes, I did."

"And you argued."

Pete looked surprised that Penelope knew all this. "Yes, we did. We argued about the blood money. He'd already paid me half, and there I was telling him I wasn't going to go through with it. I don't know which made him madder, to tell you the truth."

"So after you argued," Penelope went on, "you walked away on foot."

Pete nodded again.

"And then the next thing you know...?"

"The next thing I know," Pete whispered, "Doug's truck is bearing down on me. I'm almost home, and I get run over. And then the truck backs up, and runs over me again. And then it comes forward, and tries to run me over again, only I roll out of the way. And the truck stops. And out this guy gets and he's standing over me, and he swears to me that if I don't tell the police that Doug did this to me, he'll finish the job. And worse, he said he'd kill my sister too." Pete stopped when he ran out of breath.

And then he looked at Penelope, and even though there were tears in his eyes, he looked as if he felt better than he had in a long, long time.

"That's what happened, Penelope. I could have stopped it. Could have saved her. And I didn't."

CHAPTER 39

IT WASN'T PETE.

It wasn't Doug.

So of course, that brought Penelope round full circle again. Who killed Camille?

Michael Findley.

The County Correctional Facility was a modestly sized jail a few towns away from Franklin. And although the trip didn't take her too long, Penelope dreaded it. This was the last part of the whole investigation. She had the picture clearly now, and it sickened her.

Penelope had called ahead so that the staff would know she was coming. After securing her duty belt in her cruiser's trunk, she was buzzed through the double set of entry doors. She showed the desk officer her department ID and then signed the login sheet. There were layers of security here. For good reason. Every once in a while, they housed someone truly evil.

Penelope was shown to an interview room that was smaller than the one they used at the Franklin Police station, with a small metal table that had a single chair on either side. She took her seat. And then waited for the Correctional Officers to bring the other person to her.

When he was brought in, Michael Findley was wearing an orange jumpsuit. He was shackled at his waist and his feet. Penelope would have felt thrilled to see him finally trussed up like the animal he was, but there was no victory here.

"Sit down, Mr. Findley," Penelope said as the officers made him sit anyway and then secured him to the iron rung in the floor. "Thanks guys," Penelope said to them. "You can leave me with him. I'll let you know when I'm done."

The two guards nodded, looking uncomfortable about it, but they left anyway.

Findley sat where he was, glaring at Penelope. "I don't want to talk to you."

"Good. Excellent. Fantastic," Penelope said. "I don't want you to talk to me. In fact, you'd be doing me a favor if you sit there through this whole chat and just don't speak at all. Okay?"

Penelope knew she couldn't interview Findley. Once charged with a crime and arraigned before a judge, the right to an attorney automatically attached to a person.

Without Findley's lawyer present, nothing he said in answer to any of Penelope's questions could be used in court against him. But Penelope didn't want to ask him any questions.

Penelope wanted to put this thing to rest.

"So, Mr. Findley," she said. "First things first. You've been charged in the attempted murder of Pete Lamb. You know that. You should also know that Pete is home from the hospital and has made a full statement about what you did to him. A full statement," she emphasized.

Findley's eyes narrowed.

"That's right. So he's also told us about how you paid him to murder Camille. About how he couldn't go through with it. About how you two argued over that and how that was why you tried to kill him, and then threatened to kill his sister if he talked."

Findley snickered. "Still doesn't say I killed her, officer. Guess you're out of suspects."

Penelope just smiled. "Pretty sure I asked you to sit there and be quiet. See, Pete's confession to what he'd almost done showed us where to look. Where does a guy like you come up with all that cash, anyway? Don't answer that. I can't ask you questions in here, and I know where it came from anyway. That bank in California's going to be happy to know they can at least get some of their money back."

Findley glared daggers.

"You see, the serial numbers on the bills you paid

Pete to kill Camille matched those from the California bank job. Not too smart."

So we figured that part out, and Pete didn't know your name, but you are pretty identifiable. What with that crooked nose and that snake tattoo, and all. Pete picked you out of a photo lineup easily. And so did Dan Hughes. You nearly killed him, but he lived, so that would be attempted murder charge two."

A low sound, similar to a snarl, bubbled up from deep in Findley's throat.

"So," Penelope went on. "That led us to look into how you got from Franklin, where you were on Friday, back to Gainesville on Saturday night to kill Camille. See, we knew she was still alive on Saturday morning because she dropped Trevor off to his father. To Doug. Didn't expect her to do that, did you?"

Findley didn't answer, which was fine with Penelope.

"There's a taxi service in Gainesville. Paul's Livery, it's called. They made a run on Saturday night from Franklin to Gainesville and then back again. To your apartment building, to be precise. The driver recognized you in that same photo lineup. Pretty gutsy, I got to say, to take a taxi over to kill your girlfriend. You may possibly be the most arrogant...person I've ever met."

Penelope looked into the eyes of the monster sitting across from her. There was nothing there. No trace of humanity. No love. No regret. Only hatred. Only evil.

"So anyway. That's what I came to tell you, Mr.

Findley. I came to tell you that we've got you dead to rights, so to speak. Funny I should use that term, isn't it? I mean, with Florida being a death penalty state, and all? Know what I would do, if I were you?" Penelope stood up and went to the door of the interview room, pushing the button to signal the control room she was done. "If I were you, I'd take whatever deal they offered me and confess to everything I did. If you wanted to save your worthless life, that is."

As the door buzzed open, Penelope had the satisfaction of seeing Findley slump forward in his chair, finally realizing he was beat.

And there it was, finally. The last piece of the puzzle put in place.

CHAPTER 40

"SO THAT'S IT Chief," Penelope finished explaining to Chief Jackson as they sat in his office a few hours later. "It's a little twisted, I know, but the fact is that Michael Findley paid Pete to kill Camille, tried to kill him when he didn't go through with it, and then forced him to frame Doug."

"Okay," the Chief said, leafing through the folder on the case that Penelope had handed to him. "And then when Pete wouldn't do it, Findley killed Camille himself. I'm following that much. But the question still remains, why did Findley want Camille dead? And why frame Doug?"

"Well, I'm only guessing at part of this, but I'm thinking that Camille found out that Michael was wanted in California for that armed robbery. She said as much to Doug when she dropped their son off to him, just before she was murdered. I think she was going to turn him in and knew it might get sticky, so she wanted to keep Trevor safe. When Findley found out what she was going to do to him, he killed her."

"And he didn't want to be arrested for murder, so he tried to get our local town drunk to do it, knowing he needed money that badly?" the Chief put that next part together before Penelope could say it. "Okay, I'm with you this far. But why our town drunk? Why not someone from over in Gainesville?"

"Because of something Findley actually admitted to. Camille was going to leave him for Doug, and Findley knew it. So he wanted to take Doug down at the same time, because nobody takes away what's his—at least in his mind. He found someone in Doug's hometown to do the job, and found a way to pin it on Doug. And it all would have worked out, if not for some pretty courageous people who did the right thing in spite of being faced with some pretty definite evil."

The Chief closed the folder. "I'd say it was more than that. I'd say Findley would have definitely gotten away with it, if not for you."

"If not for God's guidance and grace, you mean." Penelope took the folder back. "I'm just the instrument here."

"Your faith in God is what makes you who you are, Penelope. I know that." He smiled and reached a hand out to Penelope. "I know that I'll be turning these reins over to the right person when I step down."

"I still can't believe you're retiring." The Franklin Police station without Curtis Jackson. Hard to imagine, Penelope thought.

"Oh, it's time for me to go, Penelope. Got a nice little retirement home down in the Keys that the wife and I are going to move to and live out our years together. We're ready. I hope you're ready too."

"Well, it depends on how soon you're going."

"I've got a date all set. You've got time to get ready."

"How long?"

"Two months," the Chief said. "Plenty of time."

Penelope laughed, and Curtis laughed with her. Two months? Considering all that had happened over the last four days, anything could happen in the next two months.

Hours of paperwork still faced Penelope. In spite of why Pete did what he did, he had still taken money to murder someone. The fact that he didn't go through with it didn't mean it wasn't still a crime. Ultimately, that case would be turned over to the District Attorney's office, and they would decide what to do with Pete. Penelope hoped there would be some leniency for Pete considering how he was cooperating now. But Penelope still had to do her part of it and cross all of the T's and dot all of the I's first. And now there were more charges to put on Michael Findley's head—the murder of his girlfriend, the attempted murder of Pete and the assault on Dan

Hughes among them.

No one in Franklin would ever see Michael Findley again in his natural life. Ever. He was going to be put away for several lifetimes, if not longer.

* * *

Later that night, when she finally got home, she was pleasantly surprised to find Jacob waiting for her, sitting on her front porch. He was wearing blue jeans and a black t-shirt that flattered his wide shoulders and muscular arms. The smile he gave her as she got out of her car warmed her heart.

"Hi there, officer beautiful," he said. He stood as she got closer, and held her in his arms in a tight embrace. "I understand you've had a long day."

"I have," she told him, breathing in the subtle scent of his cologne, citrus and honey with a hint of coriander. "Did Doug tell you everything?"

He nodded, stepping back a bit to place his hands on the sides of her face and look into her emerald eyes. "He did. Are you okay?"

He always knew her so well. "Yes, baby, I'm okay."

"You know, Doug told me something else, too. He told me you finally laid down your burden."

"I did," she said, taking hold of his hands with her own. "Finally, after all these years, that guilt is gone. I'm not carrying it around inside me anymore."

"I can tell, Penny. There's a certain calmness about you."

"I guess there is."

She led him to the door but he stopped her before she could open it. Leaning down to her, he kissed her lips, a deep kiss full of love and reassurance. "I love you," he said to her, his lips still against hers.

"I love you back," she answered.

Just then the door flew open and little Trevor stood there. "Auntie Penny!" the boy shouted, jumping up into Penelope's arms, ready or not. "I love you too, Auntie Penny. And so does God."

Penelope's heart swelled at Trevor's simple words. This was what family was about. This was what her parents' sacrifice had been about, even. Love. Unconditional love that came from deep inside, from the strength and reserve that God allowed all who relied on Him to experience.

That strength got Penelope through the most trying case of her career. It had allowed her to free a friend of false accusation. And, it had allowed her to finally release the bad feelings pent up inside of her over her parents' death. She was ready, now, to take on the mantle of being a wife and mother—truly ready. She could use her parents' good example now, and give herself completely to Jacob. Start a family with him, without the fear and guilt of her childhood marring the experiences they would have together.

During her evening prayers, she was able to thank

God for so much. And she was able to finally thank her parents for their sacrifice that had allowed her to live.

"Thank you Mom. Thank you, Dad. I hope to live up to your example someday. I hope I've made you proud."

She went to sleep that night without the heavy heart that had weighed her down for so many years. A feeling of peace settled over her and she knew, somehow, that her parents were proud of her.

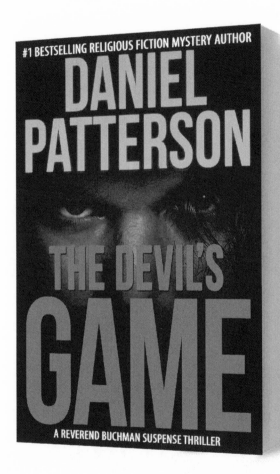

#1 BESTSELLING RELIGIOUS FICTION MYSTERY AUTHOR

DANIEL PATTERSON

THE DEVIL'S GAME

A REVEREND BUCHMAN SUSPENSE THRILLER

THE LATEST THRILLER FROM BESTSELLING
AUTHOR DANIEL PATTERSON

DANIEL PATTERSON is the author of the #1 bestselling religious fiction mystery, One Chance. Before turning his attention to writing, Daniel spent his days working as an executive in the Internet industry. A San Francisco native, Daniel currently resides in Southern California where he is busy working on the next book in the *Penelope Chance Mystery Series.*

Made in the USA
Lexington, KY
12 January 2015